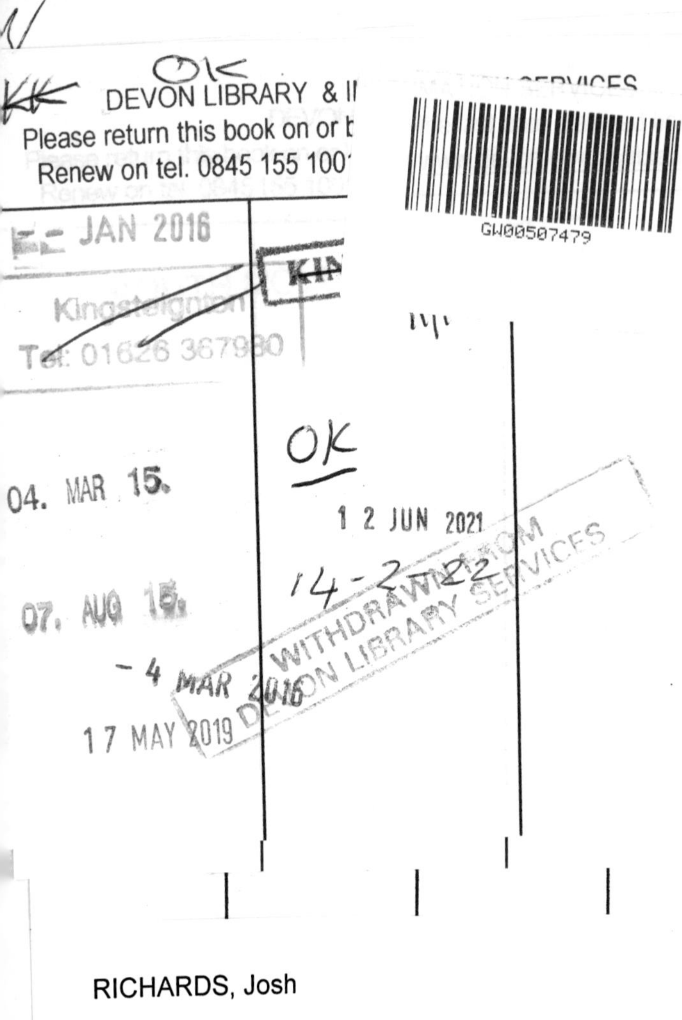

RICHARDS, Josh

Colt harvest

Colt Harvest

Like all the Old Man's boys, Ron Purcell was a tough *hombre* but that day he felt fear and premonition in his bones. Where had all the Loop V cattle gone? Ron's search for the steers led him to Hank who shared a cabin with Walt. But there was no Walt and Hank was lying dead, a bullet hole in his forehead. Worse still, when Ron reported the murder to Sheriff Brighouse, in Rampage City, he was to discover Walt with his throat cut from ear to ear.

And then there was Ron's old friend Kid Stone who had mysteriously arrived in town as a faro-dealer. What was the young trouble-shooting gambler to do with the drunken Sheriff Brighouse?

There were mysteries a-plenty to be solved but before the guns were silent again, death by flying lead would strike both Rampage City and the Loop V ranch. Would the fighting never cease?

Colt Harvest

Josh Richards

ROBERT HALE · LONDON

First hardcover edition 2003
Originally published in paperback
as *Colt Harvest* by Vern Hanson

ISBN 0 7090 7272 4

Robert Hale Limited
Clerkenwell House
Clerkenwell Green
London EC1R 0HT

All characters in this story are entirely fictitious and have no relation to any living person

Typeset by
Derek Doyle & Associates, Liverpool.
Printed and bound in Great Britain by
Antony Rowe Limited, Wiltshire

CHAPTER I

Ron Purcell halted his mount and rose in the stirrups, shading his eyes with one hand as he looked about him. He was a little alarmed. Although there was plenty of evidence of cattle having been here, there was not a single steer in sight. The grass danced mockingly around him and finally he lowered his head, weary of pitting his eyesight against the baleful glare of the sun.

The Loop V was a huge spread and the Mud Hollow line-hut at its uttermost boundary. Ron had been glad when he came in sight of the clump of stunted cottonwoods on the rim of the hollow. He had been riding since sun-up in order to take over the duties of one of the line-riders before the day got too long in the tooth. He had not had much breakfast because the cook back at the ranch had objected to getting up even half-an-hour before his usual time. Ron had long since used up all the water and biscuits he had brought with him; he figured there would be a meal fixed for him at the little cabin.

Now his anticipation was tempered by sudden

alarm, almost a premonition of evil. The tiny valley ahead of him had once been a buffalo-wallow, hence its name. The two old pardners, Walt Crisp and Hank Butler, had been the main men there, off and on, ever since Mud Hollow became Loop V property. But now Walt, the oldest of the two, had fallen sick and been taken into town for doctoring. Ron was to take his place. Ron was glad of the chance; he liked the other member of the duo, phlegmatic, walrus-moustached Hank Butler.

Ron was tall, lean and rangy, with flowing brown hair and a set to his shoulders which betokened him a handy man to have around in a fight. He was twenty-seven years old and maybe would not have looked that if it was not for the long scar down one side of his handsome face, giving it, in repose, an almost Satanic look. Now it was set, his eyes almost hidden beneath troubled brows, as he let himself slump once more in the saddle.

It was strange that there were not any cattle hereabouts, not a single one. They usually kept to this side of the dip because the grazing was better; the other side was almost on the edge of the badlands that reached clear to the border. Maybe something had scared them away – a rampaging wildcat or something. Ron could tell nothing from the jumbled tracks. Maybe old Hank was already round there, needing help to drive the critturs back to the best pasture. It was clear, though, if the cattle were being hazed, that Ron could not hear anything of them.

He remembered something that had happened a

couple of years back when he first started to work for the Loop V. There had been a terrific storm and a bunch of cattle in this section of the range had stampeded in terror. They had rolled into Mud Hollow and fetched one wall of the cabin down, almost killing one of the men inside it. Lucky for old Walt and Hank, they had been on a spell off-duty at that particular time. The wholesale opinion at the ranch was that the hollow was a dangerous place to have a line hut. It was a trap, as well as being pretty doggoned damp in the rainy season. But the Old Man was too miserly to have the cabin and etceteras moved in to the flat: he had the wall rebuilt and the cabin remained where it was. Walt and Hank always seemed pretty happy there anyway, so maybe the Old Man did right after all.

Nothing else had happened at Mud Hollow and the incident had been forgotten. But now the memory of it was brought back forcibly to Ron Purcell as he urged his horse forward once more. There was something a little ominous about the tangled tracks, the beat-up ground. There had not been any storms lately; but sometimes the slightest things sent a herd of skittish cattle into a stomping panic.

The young waddy reined-in his horse again in the meagre shade of the cottonwoods and looked down into the tiny valley drowsing in the sunshine. There was no sign of life. No smoke curled from the stack of the little cabin. The tiny corral was empty of horseflesh. The pool in the centre glistened in the sunshine like a large mirror. The buffalo-wallow had been cleared, dug deeper, and now there was a clear spring. Ordinarily the scene would have been an idyllic one, but now, to Ron Purcell, there was something ominous about the very peace and quietness.

With a gentle pressure of his knees he eased his horse down the slope. His upper body, however, was taut. He held the reins with his left hand; his other was on the gun at his hip, the holster tied to his thigh by a whang-string. Even though he inwardly jeered at himself for being spooked at nothing, his native caution, engendered by years of riding lawless trails, prevented his sinews from paying any attention to his mind.

Maybe Hank was out on a little round-up, had taken his pack-horse with him, too, hence the emptiness of the corral. Maybe Hank had been so worried about the cattle that he had forgotten all about Ron's impending arrival; maybe he had left a note in the cabin . . .

Maybe. *Maybe* . . .

Ron's horse shied violently. They were almost at the bottom of the slope. Ron was jerked backwards, almost flung from the saddle. He held on grimly with one hand. His gun was already in his other one, drawn with lightning swiftness, a purely reflex action. There was nothing at all to shoot at!

The horse's hooves scrabbled frantically on the slope, starting a miniature landslide and sending up clouds of dust. Snorting, the beast backed away from a patch of coarse long grass which, at a glance, looked quite innocent. Ron drew the beast to one side, gentling it with his hand, speaking soothing words into its ear.

Finally the horse was still and, gun in hand, Ron dismounted. He advanced cautiously on the patch of long grass; maybe a rattler was lurking there.

He saw something and raised his gun; then lowered it again. The thing he saw was the sole of a riding boot, the toe digging into soft soil at the base of the grass.

In a second Ron stood over the man who lay face downwards, almost hidden.

There was death there. Ron had seen it too many times before to mistake it now. Even before he turned the body over he knew it was that of Hank Butler.

When he saw the face he did not want to look at it any more. The handsome walrus moustache was bedraggled with drying blood; a heavy slug had smashed into Hank's forehead at close range.

Ron, because of earlier training in the lawless school of the Frontier, was probably less squeamish than most men of his age. But this was somebody he had known, rode with, joked with, a man he had liked very much.

He forced himself to feel among the clothing, to roll the body over again. In Hank's pitiful possessions – the plug of tobacco, the jack-knife, the few coins – there was no clue.

Ron inspected the ground around the body and found nothing. Hank's holster was empty and his gun was nowhere near. Ron made a clicking noise with his tongue. His horse, skirting the body widely, began to follow him as he walked slowly towards the cabin.

So great had been the impact of Ron's discovery upon him, and his anxiety to find some clue, anything to go upon, he had not realized until now that the killer might still be lurking around.

He was right in the open now and could not turn back. He waited for the horse to catch up with him and walked beside the beast, taking a little cover. His body prickled with tension, but he walked effortlessly, letting his gun swing at his side. He reached the cabin without mishap, then swerved to the side of it instead of approaching the door or the window. The horse stood uncertainly at the corner.

Ron pressed his ear to the log wall. There was no sound from inside the cabin. He moved around the back of it, soundlessly, and stopped to listen again. He went on, right round the cabin until he was at the window.

The interior was dim and he could not see anybody there. He ducked and ran beneath the window. He reached the door, put a hand out, lifted the latch. He lashed out with one booted foot and the door flew open with a crash. Nothing else happened. Feeling a little foolish, he walked into the cabin.

It was, as usual, neat and clean. Both Hank and Walt had seen service in the Civil War and they kept their billet and belongings the way old soldiers should.

Ron went to the door again and looked upwards and around at the rim of the tiny valley. He tried to think dispassionately, to figure out how, exactly, Hank had met his death. Only a supposed friend, somebody the walrus-moustached oldster knew and trusted, could have got that close to him on the slope. But what skunk could have shot him in such a cowardly way, and why?

Then again, Hank could have been shot as he breasted the rim up there by the cottonwoods. He could have tumbled down to where he lay; the shifting surface of the slope would have left little evidence of this.

Ron went back to the spot to investigate. He climbed the slope to the cottonwoods but found nothing. He retraced his steps and lifted Hank Butler's body gently in his arms and carried it to the cabin. There he laid it on one of the bunks and covered it with the blanket. He found the key and locked the door behind him before leaving the place. This was probably the first time it had been locked since the two old-timers took up residence there.

He filled his canteen at the spring. The horse had already taken his fill there; Ron mounted him, urged him up the slope once more. Man and horse began to skirt the small basin as they followed the tracks of the herd.

The cattle had gone right around the edge of Mud Hollow and on to the other side. The tracks led on from there, out into the badlands.

It was on the edge of the badlands that Ron found the sombrero.

It had been pounded considerably by sharp hooves but still retained some of its former glory. It was of soft felt; black, unusually wide-brimmed, even for a Mexican-style sombrero. Fragments of an ornate lizard-skin band still adhered to it.

Ron punched it out and tried it on his own head. It came down over his ears; it must have belonged to a giant of a man.

He went on a little further. The tracks of the herd led straight out across the badlands, straight out to where small peaks shimmered in the heat-haze. Here was the border of Mexico and no doubt a market for the stolen cattle. A callous killing, a cool rustling haul; and the only clue a battered black sombrero.

CHAPTER II

Ron knew it was no use continuing alone. Once he got on the other side of the border he would be in unfamiliar territory. The only thing to do was to bring somebody out who knew it; Charlie Pinto, half-Indian wrangler back at the ranch, for instance.

Ron turned his horse about. He descended into Mud Hollow again. He tied old Hank's body across the front of the saddle and set off back to the ranch. The line-hut and the rest would be all right. There was nothing worth stealing from there now anyway – the rustlers had seen to that.

Ron wondered if they had been a Mexican band.

The Mexicans in this particular section of the border were simple, peaceable farmers. There had not been any rustling here for years. The last batch of cattle-stealing, which had happened long before Ron hit the territory, had led to a range war. And crooked Americans had been at the back of all this.

Maybe the rustlers would return. Maybe the black sombrero would prove to be a stronger clue than he had at first thought.

He remembered something Burt Cooley, the Loop V ramrod had said some time back: that Mud Hollow was an easy pitch for a bunch of rustlers. And the Old Man had replied, in that special scoffing voice he used sometimes, that rustlers knew better than to show their faces around the Loop V any more, that he (he spoke as if he had done the job himself, single-handed) had driven the last of 'em out years ago.

Well, once more it looked like the bullheaded old cuss had been proven wrong. It was funny now how much Ron remembered about the Old Man and his bullheaded tantrums. And when he looked down at the still figure across the front of his saddle, he almost began to hate his boss. If the line-hut had been taken out of Mud Hollow as suggested, probably the rustlers would not have been able to creep up the way they did, and even if they had eventually gotten away with the cattle, maybe Hank would've escaped with his life . . .

Yeh, the Old Man and his bullheadedness had a few things to answer for all right.

The ranch buildings were dazzlingly white in the sunshine. It hurt a man's eyes to look at them. The Old Man had had everything painted that way years ago to match the imposing 'dobe and clapboard ranchhouse. They had a fresh coat every year, sometimes twice if the Northers had been particularly fierce.

As Ron spurred his horse down the slope into the wide lush valley a man crossed the yard and disappeared into one of the buildings.

The ranch squatted somnolently once more. Ron was not fooled, however. As he hit the flat he slowed his horse, cupped his hand around his mouth and gave a hail.

Jake, the fat cook, came out of his domain idly swinging a shotgun in one hand. Charlie Pinto, the wrangler, appeared from behind the stables, his hand still lurking near the butt of his gun. Behind him, half-hidden by the shadows, was his assistant, the taciturn Indian boy they called 'Happy'.

Two more men appeared from nowhere, stood immobile now, thumbs hooked in belts. Ron knew all of them had been watching him for some time and had not showed themselves until they were certain who he was or, in fact, until he gave a holler. The Old Man was a suspicious old buzzard and he liked his men to be the same or, at least, act that way. The Old Man had built his empire on eternal vigilance, on shooting first and asking questions afterwards. There were lot of folks still who coveted that empire and the Old Man wasn't aiming to give them a chance to nibble at it.

The men began to come out now, the fluctuating skeleton staff that was always kept back at the ranch, lackeys most of them, except for Jake and Charlie Pinto, and Happy and the two waddies, who had probably done a double night-turn or something and had been catching up on their rest.

They gathered around him now and gently inspected the body on the horse while, dismounting, the young man told his story.

Suddenly one of them said, 'The Ol' Man's waitin',' and all eyes were turned towards the ranch-house.

He stood on the veranda, leaning on his stick, looking towards them, immobile. Ron led his horse across there. The others melted, went back to their affairs.

He was like a very old and rather bedraggled eagle. His snow-white hair stuck up on his head in wiry tufts and his walrus moustache, of the same colour, badly needed clipping. You could not see his mouth, only his bony and aggressive chin. His nose, too, a bronzed beak and the eyes above it like chips of blue ice. They could be unbelievably frosty or they could fill with fire. The Old Man was of medium height and pretty scrawny at that. Old soldier that he was, his back was straight as a ramrod. Nobody knew his right age. Some said seventy, some said nearer to eighty. He didn't *have* to be big in stature – there was something big about him. He was a pretty awe-inspiring old cuss.

His eyes were frosty now, his voice had a metallic rasp as he asked, 'Who is it?'

Ron Purcell had stopped being scared years ago, of man or beast, old or young. He had seen the Old Man strike a cowhand with his stick once. Maybe that was the only reason he carried a stick; he certainly didn't need it to lean on. Ron knew that if the old man ever attempted to strike him, the old goat would never live to be the hundred he always bragged about aiming at.

He answered the Old Man's question. The stick went thump-thump twice on the veranda boards.

The Old Man wanted to know more. Ron told him all of it.

He said, finally, 'I thought mebbe if I took Charlie Pinto with me we might pick up a trail, if it's not too old. One of the others could ride in for the law.'

'We don't need the law,' said the Old Man. He eyed Ron keenly. 'Yeh, you take Charlie Pinto an' those two other boys who're dragging their tails around here. If you don't find anything you can call in town *afterwards* an' tell the law. But I don't want any interferin' from that badge-totin' sheepherder, Sam Brighouse, y'understand?'

'Yeh, boss. What will I do with Hank?'

'Lie him down here on the veranda. I'll get things done. I'll say the service over him myself.'

Ron unhitched the body, carried it up the steps, laid it almost at the old man's feet. An offering, he thought sardonically. He wondered if the old buzzard felt any grief about Hank, who had been with him for so many years, or was it just his pride that was making him mad that somebody should dare to shoot a Loop V hand!

He could tell nothing from the Old Man's face. He left him there, leaning on his stick. Maybe he was looking down at old Hank now: Ron did not turn his head to find out.

He rounded up Charlie Pinto and the other two boys. He got himself a fresh horse and some water and chow. Then they set out.

Charlie rode a horse like he was part of it, though he was so brown and wizened most beasts dwarfed him almost ludicrously. Yet he had a strange control over them. The other two men were of about Ron's age. Duke Linstone was small and dark and dandified. Pete Manetti was dark, too, but taller and thinner, much thinner. His well-worn clothes seemed to hang on him. His gun and holster were well-worn, too, well-greased. He talked little and had the reputation of a gunfighter.

The Old Man picked his boys well. Ron Purcell with his flowing brown hair and his scar, his reputation as a trouble-shooter. Duke, who lived up to his name, but was a handy man to have around in a pinch. Manetti with his itching trigger-finger. Pinto who had once slit a man's throat for mistreating a horse. An ill-assorted bunch maybe, but strangely of a pattern: dangerous men used to dangerous trails. They were all of that kind, the Old Man's boys: from Burt Cooley, the ramrod, and downwards; if there was actually any *downwards*, for the Old Man did not suffer fools . . .

The quartet reached the rim of Mud Hollow and Charlie Pinto began his perigrinations in search of signs. He led them right around the edge of the hollow, then down into it.

He expressed the view laconically that there had been a sizeable bunch of rustlers. He then led his companions out on to the edge of the badlands and began to pick up the trail which Ron Purcell, not being half Indian and half-fox, had completely missed.

It was here that Ron bethought himself of the black sombrero which, what with his chat with the Old Man and the subsequent haste, he had completely forgotten. Pinto unfolded the hat, punched it into shape. 'I don't think it's a real Mex hat,' he said. 'Not made in Mexico I mean.'

'That's what I figured,' said Ron.

'Let me take a look,' said Duke and Pinto leered and handed it over to him.

Duke inspected it with the air of a connoisseur. 'It's good stuff,' he said. 'Probably cost quite a bit. What's left o' the band is real lizard-skin. I'm inclined to agree with you about the other thing though. It was probably bought this side of the border by a man who likes fancy dressing.' He put his head on one side. 'Not a well-dressed man maybe, not a man who knows how to dress properly, but one who just likes flashy things.'

'Like you,' drawled Pete Manetti.

Duke glared at him. 'No, not like me, oakhead,' he snapped.

'Wal, you should know,' said Pete and winked at the other two. Pete could be funny at times – and usually at his dandified pardner's expense.

Duke snorted disdainfully and handed the hat back to Ron. They went on.

Presently they hit a stretch of that freak rock formation that one comes across in the desert here and there. Pinto halted them and went on ahead alone. For a while him and his horse seemed to be doing some kind of squaredance against the setting sun. But finally he came back.

'Looks like the trail's petered out,' he growled. He didn't like being beaten. 'But we'll go on for a while. May be able to pick it up again.'

'A herd of cattle just cain't vanish into thin air,' said Ron Purcell.

But he had to admit about half an hour later that that was just what they seemed to have done.

CHAPTER III

It was dark when the little party reached Rampage City. They had called in at Mud Hollow on their way back from the badlands and stayed there a while, trying to find more clues, chewing things over while they had some chow. But by now they were hungry again and made a bee-line for the nearest eating-house.

This little jumbled township in a shallow basin in the cow-country stood on the site of an Indian massacre. Here a pioneer waggon-train had come to rest, folks had pitched their tents, begun to build their homes. A war-party of Indian bucks, rampaging on white man's fire water had descended on them one weary night, slaughtering men and women and children, taking away the young girls to suffer unmentionable horrors.

The sons of those braves had been driven away from the territory long since but the horrible story still lingered, remembered even among the bloodier and more notorious ones. Another settlement had sprung up on the bloodsoaked soil of the basin.

Rampage City, so aptly named by some perverted humorist. But the title had stuck. Rampage City grew and prospered, not good, not particularly bad, the prototype of dozens of such towns the length and breadth of the lusty South-west.

It had its saloons, its dance-halls, its bawdy houses, its hash-houses; one church, one bank, one town-hall, one dog-catcher, one town drunk, one sheriff . . . But it was characteristic of the Loop V boys that they did not give this last-named character a thought until they had filled their bellies with food and drink.

Then they ambled down to the jail-house, only to find it in darkness. Ron Purcell hammered on the door marked Sheriff's Office. Private. There was no answer.

'The first time I've been near the doggoned place in six months. You'd think they'd welcome me better'n this.' Ron grinned.

'That goes for me an' Pete, too,' said Duke Linstone.

'I was here 'bout a month ago,' put in Charlie Pinto. 'Sam Brighouse was hitting the bottle pretty heavily then. I guess he's in one o' the saloons right now.'

'It's time the ol' buzzard was pensioned off,' said Duke.

'Yeh, but who'd take his place? The law's kind of a laughing stock hereabouts y' know an' nobody likes to be laughed at. Out there,' Charlie jerked a crooked arm, 'the Old Man runs everything – and here in Rampage Lemmy Macklein does the ramrodding ... Come to think of it, mebbe Sam's in Lemmy's place right now. Lemmy's boys seem to like plying Sam with drinks just for the fun of seeing him slobber.'

'That pleases their boss no doubt,' said Ron Purcell. 'He more than anybody has helped to make the law a laughing stock in Rampage.'

'Wal, what're we waiting for?' said Pete Manetti, speaking for the first time in the last half hour or so. 'Let's go to Lemmy's place.'

Its proper name was The Golden Lizard but all the Rampage regulars called it Lemmy's Place. The Golden Lizard might seem like a good name to a fancy Eastern gambler like Lemmy Macklein, but it was kind of amusing to the local roughnecks – though none of them were silly enough to say so in front of the snake-like Lemmy or any of his cohorts.

The frontage of The Golden Lizard was not a flimsy false one but had the whole three storeys packed solidly behind it. An imposing front at that; red, black and white with letters three feet high, the whole façade festooned with naphtha flares. The lower front windows were wide and uncurtained, throwing out a welcoming glow. The side and upstairs windows were discreetly curtained for the convenience of gambling schools, and gentry who liked private rooms in which to entertain their girl-friends – the latter usually supplied by the management.

Girls could be heard squealing and laughing now; there was the clank of a piano, the strains of a concertina, guitar and fiddle, the stamping of feet, the loud voices of men. The air which came through the gaily ornamented batwings was warm, cloying, redolent of sweat, liquor, cheap scent and smoke. The four men spread out a little as they entered, looked about them.

The place was packed. Smoke hung in a blue cloud around the chandeliers. The light was dazzling-bright after the darkness outside. One or two people spoke to the pardners as they began to work their way through the crowd.

Duke Linstone signalled to Ron Purcell; his mouth formed the words, 'There he is.'

There he was indeed; the word was passed along and the four men converged on the bar and Sheriff Sam Brighouse. The sheriff's whole attention was concentrated on the dregs in the bottom of his glass until Duke said, 'Have another one, Sam.'

The sheriff turned slowly, blinking owlishly. 'Oh, hullo, Duke . . . Hullo, boys.' The bartender was at his elbow, he pushed the glass across and had it filled. Duke held up four fingers. Four more drinks were soon forthcoming.

'After you've finished that one, Sam, we'd like to see you in your office,' said Ron Purcell.

'Office's closed,' said Sam thickly.

'You better open it again,' said Pete Manetti, his tone a little ugly.

The sheriff did not seem to notice this. He had emptied his glass again. He pushed it across the bar, motioned to the barman.

'You've had enough, Sam,' said Ron Purcell. 'Come on. This is important.'

'Don't crowd me,' said the sheriff. He looked ludicrously pugnacious, with his sagging belly, his mournful grey walrus moustache, his jaw out-thrust like that of a petulant child.

But Pete Manetti was already crowding him, edging him away from the bar. He snatched the other drink, downed it so quickly that some of the liquor ran down his unshaven chin. He was so far away from the bar that he could not reach it. He let the empty glass fall with a tinkling crash to the floor. In the general din, the shifting kaleidoscope of night life, the little incident went unnoticed. Sam was being gently but firmly jostled further away from the bar.

Pete Manetti was a little hasty and a little rough. Somebody said curtly in his ear, 'What's going on?'

Pete turned to look into the face of a lean young man in a string tie and black broadcloth. He was hatless and his hair was the colour of ripe corn; his cheeks were hollowed and bloodless, his pale blue eyes frosty. Despite himself, the tough Pete Manetti felt a shudder run through him as he met the gaze of those eyes. But he was soon himself again and enquired: 'You talking to me, mister?'

'I am.' The young man seemed to be poised on his toes. His hands were hooked into his crossed gunbelts. A two-gun man; Pete Manetti let his body sag slowly into a crouch, his hand crooked over his gun. Just one gun, well-worn: Pete was deadly, he did not need notches to boast his progress.

At his other side the voice of Ron Purcell suddenly spoke up. 'Kid! By all that's holy – Kid Stone!'

The young man's hands fell lower, his frosty eyes warmed a little as he looked past Pete. Ron Purcell's hand closed gently, reassuringly, over Pete's arm and the latter relaxed a little, too.

'Ron Purcell!' The Kid's voice was soft, velvety, but like his face, strangely expressionless. And the eyes had dulled now, too, as if ashamed of their show of warmth.

The little party had halted among the surging throng. Before either Ron or the Kid could speak again, the sheriff piped up, 'These gents want me to go to the office with them, Les. I dunno. . . .' His voice tailed off.

Ron looked from the kid to the sheriff and back again. It was a long time since he had heard Kid Stone called Les. What had the young trouble-shooting gambler to do with the drink-sodden old lawman . . . ?

But evidently the Kid was, in some way, the old man's champion. So Ron said, 'It's a pretty important thing, Kid. We need the law. We can't do much here.'

'All right, Sam. I'll come along, too.'

So Kid Stone led the way. Thin, hatless, almost boyish, his stride panther-like, his fingertips brushing his sides.

Then the gun boomed from the other side of the street and a slug thudded into the log wall in front of Kid's head. Then he was ducking, weaving, and the gun in his hand was spitting flame, drowning the other shots.

The sheriff was flat against the wall and, before

him, Ron Purcell half-crouched, a gun in his hand, too. The sidewalk positively bristled with guns now. The men had spread out, hugging the shadows. Suddenly, still crouching, Kid Stone began to run, making a sweep across the street. Ron Purcell followed his example, going in the other direction.

They met on the opposite sidewalk, shaking their heads at each other. There the other men joined them and kept watch in the street while Kid and Ron combed the two alleys opposite Lemmy's Place. As they came back, empty-handed, the saloon was disgorging people.

Swinging doors gushed light and humanity. Windows were flung open, noise came in fluctuating waves.

'Let's get rid o' these braying jackasses,' said Kid.

He pranced on to the sidewalk, waving his arms. 'It's all right, folks. I'm trigger-happy – took a shot at a cat that startled me.'

'Lot o' noise over a mangy cat,' said a big fellow.

Kid whirled to face him, poised on his toes. 'I hope you don't doubt my word, friend,' he said silkily.

The man shuffled his feet. His truculence became sheepish. 'Well, if you say it was a cat, I guess it was a cat.'

The shooting had sobered Sam Brighouse and he shambled forward now. 'It was a cat all right. Everything's all right, folks. Jest carry on.'

The four Loop V boys, coming slowly, a little menacingly, out of the half-darkness, ranged themselves behind the sheriff. The folks began to melt away, to go back to their drinking, their gaming, their dancing, their lovemaking.

'That was a mighty close call, that slug,' said Sheriff Brighouse. 'Somebody must have a grudge against you, Les.'

'That's no new story,' said the Kid laconically.

Ron Purcell wondered privately whether that slug had really been intended for the Kid. It could have been aimed at any of them: they had been pretty close together. Still, the Kid's arrogant manner, his questionable skill with cards, his reputation for a mean one had always made him plenty of enemies.

They reached the sheriff's office and old Sam unlocked the door. They passed inside. The lamp was unlit. Not until then did they realize Pete Manetti was no longer with them.

'I'll go look for him,' said Duke Linstone, in alarm. Before anybody could remonstrate, he had gone.

Ron Purcell was a little disgruntled. He would have liked to find out what had happened to Pete; and also do a little lone investigating, too, maybe. But he had to conclude that, as he had been the one to find old Hank Butler's murdered body, he should be the one to tell the story to the sheriff. This he proceeded to do. There was little the law could do that the Loop V men had not already tried. But this made the case official. The sheriff had known and liked Hank Butler. He was shocked and surprised, but, beyond that, of little help.

Ron turned towards Kid Stone, asked the young man a point-blank question. 'What brings you in this neck o' the woods, Kid?'

The palefaced gunman stiffened, looked around him at Charlie Pinto. 'I might ask you the same question.'

'I've been here two years. I work for the Loop V.'

'In what capacity?' It might've been a sneer, had not the Kid's voice been so completely expressionless.

Ron shrugged. 'Just a wet-nurse for dogies, I guess. Your turn, Kid.'

'I'm working as a faro-dealer for Lemmy Macklein.'

'A faro-dealer,' echoed Ron, softly. That was all he said.

Yeh, the Kid had always been able to do tricks with cards, to make those little spots dance to a tune of his own making. But he was one of the West's most notorious exponents of gun music, too. Was he really Sheriff Brighouse's champion or just the old man's keeper, his hand on the reins ready to jerk them if the old horse got out of line?

Ron regarded the lawman. 'Many strangers in town, Sam? Apart from Kid here, I mean?'

The old man shook his head slowly. 'Cain't recollect none.'

'I've been here almost a month,' said Kid flatly. 'Coupla hard-looking cases came into The Golden Lizard three days ago. The barman said he hadn't seen them before. They claimed to be cattle-buyers. They been out to see your boss, Ron?'

'Not that I know of,' said Ron. Charlie Pinto shook his head, too.

The sheriff spoke up suddenly, looking at Kid.

'How about that young woman who came on the stage a coupla days ago?'

Kid's eyes lit up for a moment, then dulled again. His thin lips quirked mirthlessly. 'Yeh, she was the one who rustled them cattle all right, I guess. Her and that crippled old jasper she calls Uncle.'

Brighouse blinked owlishly. He was a little slow on the uptake. 'A nice girl like her wouldn't have nothin' to do with rustling,' he said.

Everybody grinned. Then Sam flushed a little. 'Hell, you're joshing me, Les.'

'Stranger things have happened,' said Ron Purcell. 'Than lady rustlers, I mean.'

'Quit clowning,' said Brighouse, suddenly official. 'Let's get back to cases. . . .' His brow buckered. 'But there ain't nothin' we can do till daylight, is there? . . . Anyway, if Charlie here cain't find no trail o' them murdering cow-thieves I'm sure nobody else will.'

Charlie Pinto bowed ironically to the implied compliment. The sheriff brightened. 'I guess I can write out some kind of a report, though.'

'You do that,' said Ron. 'Me an' Charlie will go look for Duke an' Pete.'

'I'll stay with Sam a while,' said Kid Stone.

Ron Purcell turned slowly towards the door. Well, if the Kid wanted to stay with the sheriff he had a right to, hadn't he? Charlie followed. The door closed behind them. The night swallowed them.

CHAPTER IV

'What say we separate?' said Ron.

Charlie nodded, grunted, jerked a thumb. Ron watched his dim figure until it disappeared in an alley, then he went on himself, keeping close to the walls, yet trying not to make too much clatter with his heels on the boardwalk. After a while, however, this did not matter: he was approaching the area of the honky-tonks. There were more people around, even outdoors; and a heck of a lot more noise.

He reached Lemmy's Place, glanced through a window. Maybe Duke had met Pete and they were having a drink. He could not see them, they could be somewhere hidden among the dense smoke-encompassed throngs. He debated with himself about going inside, then finally decided against it. To look for Duke and Pete in every establishment of this kind in Rampage would be a Herculean task. Surely the two pardners would not have met and then carried on with their own affairs – drinking, gambling, wenching maybe – without looking up him and Charlie first. But you never could tell with these two: Pete, with the perpetual chip on his shoulder; Duke with his sardonic sense of humour and his weakness for the women. . . .

Ron's lean, scarred face was bathed in light for a moment. He had a wolfish look. He cursed Duke and Pete soundlessly.

He remembered suddenly old Walt Crisp, who had been brought to town for doctoring. He had croup or something. He would probably be in the little clinic in back of Doc Logan's place. Ron wondered if Pete had suddenly taken it into his head to go see Walt. Somebody would have to see the old jasper sometime, anyway, to tell him about the death of his old saddle-pal, Hank. But Ron did not think Peter would be that thoughtful.

Ron stood still for a moment, debating with himself once more. A few folks passed him, one or two glancing at him curiously, but not for long; he didn't look the kind who relished being stared at. A wolfish young hellion.

Somebody said, 'Howdy, Ron,' and he answered mechanically. A dance-hall girl approached, mincing on French stilt heels.

'Come on inside, honey,' she said, huskily. 'Have some fun.'

'Later, sugar.' He might have been talking to a friendly cur.

She opened her mouth for a pungent retort, then changed her mind. She shivered a little, flounced on into Lemmy's Place.

Ron Purcell made up his mind and went on. He

passed out of the orbit of the bright lights and reached the rambling old frame house where Doc Logan lived. Light speared through curtain slits in the parlour-window. Ron climbed up to the stoop and rapped on the door.

The Doc's wife opened it, a plump, motherly body.

'Hullo, Mr Purcell. I guess you've come to visit that ornery old friend of yours, huh?' She held open the door invitingly.

Ron stepped in. 'Yes, ma'am. Anybody else been here from the ranch?'

'I don't think so. Go in to the doc.'

The old medico was sprawled in an armchair, his boots off, his sparse white hair sticking up on his head like a turkey-cock's. He twisted his head, grinned at Ron over the back of the chair. 'Jesophat, I thought it was another customer. I've just about had my fill for one day.'

'Where's Walt, Doc?'

The old man jerked a thumb. 'In the back place. The little room. He's raring to go. Want me to take you?'

'No, that's all right. I know the way. I'd kinda like to surprise the ol' coot.'

Ron made his way through the kitchen and along the covered, lamplit passage to the outhouses which formed the philanthropic doctor's clinic-cum-hospital. He opened the door, moved along the lamplit corridor, gently opened the door at the end.

Darkness greeted him. There was no sound. Probably Walt had heard him and was playing possum.

He opened the door wider. 'Wake up, you old skunk.'

There was no answer, no sound of breathing. The hanging lantern in the passage threw light a little way into the room. Ron saw the neatly-woven rug mat, the bottom of the small white truckle bed.

'Walt,' he said, 'Walt,' and found his voice sinking to a whisper. Also his hand was at his hip and there was that familiar tight feeling in the back of his legs. His mind pooh-poohed his caution, his fear, but his muscles did not relax and he was on tiptoes as he moved out of the light, into the room. He found the nearest wall and leaned against it. Head cocked on one side, he listened. Sounds came vaguely to him from outside, from down the street. And here there was nothing. Nothing at all.

His eyes were getting accustomed to the gloom now. He could see the shape of the bed. There seemed to be somebody lying in it all right. At its head was a small table. Glass gleamed dully. Ron made two long, smooth strides across the floor. He scratched a Lucifer, lit the lamp.

He moved quickly. His draw was a thing of wonder, but there was nobody there to see it. He stood a little way from the bed, gun in hand, gazing slowly around the room. The window was open a little at the bottom. He had not noticed this before because there was no breeze and the night was warm. He went across to the window and glanced out. Nothing but scrub and gloom. He returned to the bed.

Walt Crisp lay there, the bedclothes up to his

chin. His face was a ghastly white. His teeth were bared and his eyes stared sightlessly up at the ceiling. There was blood on the white coverlet beneath his chin.

Ron reached out with his free hand and gently drew the bedclothes back.

Walt's throat had been cut from ear to ear.

Charlie Pinto had a penchant for alleys. He negotiated four of them with the utmost stealth, disturbing prowling cats and curs, three amorous couples, and a truculent drunk who had to be kicked under the chin before he would be quiet. Then, in the fifth alley, he really found something.

A sudden sound made him pause, flatten himself against the wall. The sound came again, stealthy, scrabbling. Like an animal stiffening to pounce, or a human getting in a comfortable position from which to wield a stealthy knife or gun. Charlie drew his own gun. He began to move slowly, his shoulder making a tiny whispering sound against the log wall.

He halted again as he heard something else. The sound had changed. The short hairs prickled at the back of his neck. He cocked his head on one side. The scrabbling noise came again but now there was something else: a painful, animal sound.

Charlie moved again. Then things happened with terrifying suddenness. A voice screamed a curse, a gun boomed, the noise deafening in the enclosed space. Charlie felt the slug zip past his ear as the flame blossomed. His thumb tautened on the hammer of his gun, but he held his fire: distorted by pain and rage though that voice had been, he had recognized it.

'Pete!' he yelled hoarsely. 'Pete! It's me – Charlie!'

The boom of the gun drowned the latter part of his sentence. He flung himself flat on the ground, still yelling. The echoes died away, gunsmoke drifted and tickled Charlie's throat so that he was scared he would cough or sneeze. He clenched his gun so tightly that his knuckles began to ache. Finally the voice said 'Charlie,' and he rose and went forward again. The whole thing could not have taken more than a few seconds but to Charlie it had seemed like a lifetime. He lit a match and went down on one knee beside Pete Manetti.

Pete said: 'I was slugged on the back of the head and then, when I was falling I must've twisted my ankle or somep'n. I think the skunk must've wanted to kill me without any noise. It's a good job I'm hard-headed. He should've had the sense to use a knife. When I heard you I thought it was the skunk comin' back to make sure.'

This was quite a long speech for Pete and it knocked Charlie speechless. 'Help me to get up,' growled Pete, and Charlie put an arm beneath his shoulder blades. They tottered upright, Pete hopping on one leg.

There were sounds of raised voices, coming nearer. The shooting had been heard. 'We better go this way,' said Charlie. 'Can you manage, Pete'?'

'Sure!'

Charlie helped the tall thin gunfighter to the end

of the alley and around the corner to the 'backs' of Rampage. 'We better make our way to Doc Logan's,' said Charlie. He still had his gun in his free hand. He felt like blasting away at something.

They reached the Doc's place without mishap, but were surprised to see every window blazing with light. As they clattered on to the front stoop the door was flung open and the figure of Ron Purcell was limmed against the light. He had a gun in his hand. He looked menacing, his name rose involuntarily to Charlie's lips – almost in a shout. Ron holstered his gun and came towards them. He helped Pete into the house. The only question he asked was, 'Where's Duke?' But neither of the other two men had seen the dapper cowhand since he quitted the bunch at the sheriff's office.

Doc Logan and his wife, both looking a little white and harassed, saw to Pete's leg. The lean man, without wasting words, told his story.

As the bunch had made their way to the sheriff's office after the shooting, Pete had thought he saw somebody tailing them. The man, or maybe it was more than one, had disappeared into an alley and Pete had gone after him.

He had followed the sound of the man's scuffing footsteps. The blow had caught him utterly unprepared on the back of the head. There must've been two of 'em – maybe more. Pete was surprised when he heard that Duke had gone out after him. He hadn't seen hide nor hair of the little cuss: he wanted to go out looking for him right away.

Doc Logan prodded him in the chest. 'Sit down.

You must rest that ankle or you'll collapse again. Your head isn't anything to worry about – pity the man didn't hit you a little harder, he might've knocked some sense into you.'

The jest was forced. Nobody laughed. Charlie Pinto said: 'What's been goin' on here? You all look like you've seen a ghost or somep'n.'

Ron Purcell told him what had happened.

'The killer must've gotten through the window and knifed Walt while he slept,' the scarfaced cowboy concluded. 'Mrs Logan an' Doc didn't hear a thing. I've searched around – found nothing. I'd just come in from outside when I heard you two jaspers arrive. I found marks where a horse had been standing in that small clump o' cottonwoods way back o' the house – but nothin' else.'

'What can be happening to this territory lately?' half-wailed Mrs Logan, who by now had heard of Hank Butler's death, too.

'Yes,' said her husband. 'We've had killings before, but usually in hot blood. There's something cold and evil about this business.'

'And if you ask me it's all tied in together,' said Ron Purcell. 'The murders of Hank and Walt, the bushwhack attempt outside Lemmy's Place, the attack on Pete – they're all tied up together somehow.'

'But what's behind them?' said Charlie Pinto. 'Tell me that. What's behind it all?'

'I ain't no wizard,' growled Ron. 'Come on. We better go look for Duke. I hope nothing ain't happened to him, too.'

Pete rose again but was finally persuaded to remain with Mrs Logan and the Doc and rest up a while.

'If ever I find out who slugged me,' said Pete. He didn't have to finish his sentence.

After making a tour of the town without finding Pete, and stopping in a few bars on the way to take refreshment, Duke Linstone returned to the sheriff's office. It was locked and in darkness. He went back to Lemmy's Place, thinking he'd find his partners there, or at least the sheriff and his new friend, the notorious Kid Stone.

Again he drew a blank. The snake-like Lemmy Macklein with his polished black hair was making his nightly tour, greeting the guests and suckers. But there was not even any sign of Lemmy's new faro-dealer. Duke wondered whether Kid Stone had been hired just to ramrod a faro-layout or, primarily, for something else.

Duke was a little disgruntled. Why hadn't the boys waited for him? He decided to have another drink, and wormed his way to the bar. The place was really jumping. Customers were attempting to dance with percentage-girls on the bandanna-sized floor to the tinny music of an accordion, fiddle and piano. There was not much spare room; things were getting kind of tangled. All kinds of games were going on all over the place, as well as some real plain and steady drinking.

Duke knocked back a glass of rye and called for another. A percentage-girl sidled up to his elbow.

She was dark, plump, Spanish-looking. A comely little filly. Her voice when she spoke was ripe Texan.

'Ah don't see you aroun' heah much, honah.'

Duke never could resist an attractive she-male. He preened himself. 'You're pretty new yourself aren't you?' he said aggressively.

'Ah've been heah two months.'

'Why didn't somebody tell me,' said Duke. '*Chiquita*, you an' me have some lost time to make up.'

There were tiny beads of sweat on her forehead and upper lip above the ripe red cupid's bow. She had probably been dancing with some lummoxy miner who had pushed her all over the floor. She leaned her body against Duke's with a little sigh. 'Get me a sarsasparilla, honah,' she said.

Duke was pleased that she had not asked for strong liquor. He hated women to drink that way: he was oldfashioned about them, at least in that respect.

He ordered the brown drink, and another rye for himself. All thoughts of his pardners had fled from his mind. 'Let you an' me see if we can find a table in a quiet corner.'

They took their drinks and wended their way through the packing throngs, the couples shuffling in travesties of the dance. Curious glances were thrown at them. Men greeted Duke; many winked; others leered at the girl, until hard looks from the dapper little hellion made them lower their eyes.

They found an empty table littered with glasses. The girl seemed a little uncertain. 'Looks like it belongs to somebody,' she said.

'I cain't see any Reserved tickets,' grinned Duke. 'Come on.' He pulled up the two chairs and they sat down.

The girl glanced a little apprehensively around the assembly, as if she expected some monster to come and whisk the two seats from under them.

'Relax, *chiquita*,' said the man, and she gave him a mechanical smile, began to attend to him.

'Ah heard them call you Duke. That's just a nickname ah suppose.'

'Oh, no,' said the cowboy airily. 'I come from ancient British lineage, don't y'know.' He screwed a silver dollar into his eye and grimaced at her.

She began to chuckle. There was nothing mechanical about her now. There was something about this dapper, happy-go-lucky cowpoke that was irresistible. Duke took off his hat and straightened out the creases, then replaced it on his head, pulling it over his ears. He burlesqued an English milord, or at least, a fit-up repertory company's interpretation of such, which he had seen in Abilene some years ago.

The girl went off into peals of laughter. Duke was still mugging, away, a mile a minute, when the laughter died. Her eyes widened, gazing past Duke. She half-rose.

CHAPTER V

Duke turned his head. A few yards away from him a big man stood. His face, barred by a black moustache, was a choleric red; his little eyes stared evilly at the girl, then transferred their gaze to her companion. Duke had seen him around town from time to time, but didn't know who he was, or what he was. He was dressed in conventional, well-worn cowboy garb, yet, somehow, did not have the appearance of a cowhand. Maybe he was another one of Lemmy Macklein's hard-cases. Duke did not like his looks or the way he was shooting them. 'Looking for something, friend?' the dapper waddy asked.

The hard-case showed his teeth, irregular, yellow with tobacco stain. 'You have the gall. . . !' he said. 'You sit there with my girl, at the table we generally use, an' you have the gall to ask me if I'm looking for something.'

'Ah – ah'm not your girl,' said the filly; but her voice was weak and uncertain.

The look she gave the big man was almost

appealing. 'Ah was just having a drink with this gentleman, Mose,' she said. 'After all, that is mah job.'

'*What gentleman*?' said Mose with heavy humour. He grinned and looked about him, squinting his little eyes. Duke was standing upright now, but still the other fellow dwarfed him. Duke's dark handsome face had a deceptively mild expression. His black eyebrows, as delicately scored as a woman's, rose slowly, giving him a boyish look. He glanced at the girl.

'Did you signal this galoot to come over here?' he asked flatly.

Her reply was involuntary, indignant. 'No, I didn't!'

Then she shut her mouth tightly and the colour ebbed from her face. She looked scared, looked as if she wished she hadn't spoken so quickly.

Other folks' attention was being drawn to the taut little scene. A man sniggered. Mose had the reputation of a comic. A pretty rough comic. Men waited for him to chew up this fancy pants galoot, spit him over the sawdust.

Others who knew Duke Linstone well or, at least, by reputation, were pretty sure Mose would not have things all his own way if he started anything. But Mose seemed as if he intended to take his time, give the onlookers value for money, so to speak.

Duke Linstone, however, didn't give a hoot for the big fellow's grandstand play. The dapper cowhand pranced from behind his chair, got between Mose and the girl.

'You heard the lady, friend,' said Duke. 'She didn't call you. Go back to your kennel. Wait until you're called for.'

Somebody laughed. Mose's choleric colour became a deeper shade. His little eyes almost disappeared in their red rolls of flesh. This was not right: folks were laughing in the wrong places. . . . But easy, easy – not to rush things; the boss always said he didn't like things rushed.

'The lady ain't said she didn't call me,' he said heavily.

Duke stepped a little to one side. What was between this big load of lard and the plump, dark little filly? He did not like to think there was anything between them. He gave the girl a sidelong glance. 'Tell the big fellah you didn't call him, *chiquita*,' he said flatly.

The girl's red lips worked but no sound came. The big man took a step forward. His big face looked like it was within an ace of exploding. His arm shot out, a huge red hand grasped the girl's wrist.

'You come with me,' he said. 'I'll call back an' deal with this fancy-feathered whippersnapper.'

Duke's expression did not change. He leaned across the table negligently and picked up the girl's half-filled glass of sarsasparilla and flung the contents into Mose's face.

The big man and the girl sprang apart. Mose mopped at his face with both hands, the brown liquid streaming down it, from the ends of his moustache. He was a ludicrous sight. There was more laughter, a lot of it. Duke gave a mocking little bow then, without changing his position, drove his elbow into the big man's rather large stomach. Mose went 'Oaf' and doubled over the table, completing his downfall by tipping up what was left of the rye in Duke's glass and getting that on him, too. The smell of raw liquor smote the air.

The laughter rang out, uncontrollably now.

Mose pawed at himself, gasping. He levered himself away from the table, the laughter ringing in his ears, mocking him, maddening him. He twisted, went for his gun.

'Hold it!'

Duke Linstone's voice rang savagely. There was nothing mild about his face now. It was no longer smoothly handsome either; it had a demoniacal look.

Mose's nerveless fingers lifted slowly away from the gun-butt. He saw death in the levelled .44, the dark, wicked eyes above it.

'Unbuckle the belt, fat boy,' said Duke.

Mose did as he was told, letting gun-belt and weapon fall around his feet. Duke holstered his gun, began to unbuckle his own belt. 'I don't like men who act rough with ladies,' he said. His voice was soft again now, but it rang in the sudden stillness.

Fights were common; but there was something strangely sinister and elemental about this set-up.

But now a diversion occurred. 'What's going on here?' Lemmy Macklein came forward. He could be very unobtrusive when he wished. Nobody knew from whence he had suddenly appeared. He slid forward in his snake-like way.

'Keep out of this, Macklein,' said Duke out of the corner of his mouth.

'You're not going to fight in my place,' said the saloon-keeper.

'If you don't want fights in your place you should teach your pet hoodlums better manners,' said Duke.

Mose's little eyes shifted. Lemmy was glaring at the girl. She quailed before his glance. Duke intercepted that glance. He seemed to be debating whether to slug Lemmy instead of Mose. Duke's gun-belt was on the table now, out of reach of his hand. Lemmy wore a gun in a fancy Eastern-style shoulder-holster beneath his broadcloth.

Duke drawled, 'I aim to kick the lights outa this big fraud. Whether I do it here or outside is entirely immaterial to the fact.'

'Fancy talking,' sneered Lemmy. 'I . . .'

The rest of the sentence was lost. For things began to happen then – fast! Duke was still looking at Lemmy and Mose saw his opportunity and took it. The dance-hall girl's cry of warning to Duke was drowned, too, as a chair went over with a crash. In his haste Mose had misjudged things a little. As he swung at Duke he barged against the chair. This deflected his aim somewhat; nevertheless, his ham-like list caught the dapper cowpuncher on the shoulder and sent him spinning.

Mose kicked the chair to one side, went after Duke, boot still swinging. The smaller man was down, resting on one elbow, flexing his numbed arm.

He saw the boot coming. It looked as big as a sack of molasses. He rolled swiftly, felt the wind of the heavy missile flying past his head, a breath of peril. He twisted again, grabbed a thick ankle, jerked with all his strength.

Mose, still kicking, did a neat parabola. This time he brought a table down with him – with a crash that shook The Golden Lizard to its gaudy foundations.

Duke rose, to find himself looking into the muzzle of Lemmy's fancy Eastern automatic. Mose floundered and blew weakly amid a backwash of furniture.

'Get out of here,' said Lemmy, and his voice was full of hate.

Duke ignored the gun, looking down at Mose. The big man had subsided, his eyes beginning to glaze over. His beefy face was white now except for the thread of blood running from the corner of his mouth.

Now Duke turned his attention to Lemmy. 'I've finished my chore. I'll take my gun-belt now.'

'You'll leave it right there,' said Lemmy.

Their glances locked and now Duke's dark eyes were hot with hate, too.

'You tryin' to introduce a no-gun law in your place now, Lemmy?' he asked silkily.

'With yuh, yeh!'

'The thin end of the wedge,' said Duke, and he smiled. It was not a nice smile.

But Lemmy Macklein was not a nice man and did not scare easily.

'Fancy talking,' he said again. 'Get out of here!'

Duke made a slight movement towards his gun-belt. Lemmy jerked the automatic. 'I'm warning you! You wouldn't be so pretty with a slug in your belly.'

Duke shrugged, glanced towards the girl. She still stood as though petrified, looking at nothing in particular. He felt sorry for her. If he found out that Lemmy or Mose had taken it out of her afterwards because of him, there'd be trouble. There'd be trouble anyway: Mose could be dismissed, but Duke aimed to take things up with Lemmy later. There was little he could do now in the face of a levelled gun, unless he wanted to commit a particularly messy kind of suicide. He shuddered at the thought of his nice outfit being all daubed up with his own rich blood. He had aimed to come into town today – though not under the same circumstances as had ultimately transpired – so had togged himself out accordingly.

He shrugged again. He winked at the girl, treating the levelled gun with profound contempt. '*Adios, chiquita.*'

'*Adios*, Duke.' Her voice was little more than a husky whisper.

Lemmy glared at her. Duke was level with him, seemed to have all his interest centred on the door, on getting out of here before he got shot at. But a relaxation of Lemmy's vigilance had been what Duke was angling for: this had been in his mind when he attempted the little byplay with the girl.

He swung now, as if on a pivot, and with almost unbelievable swiftness. He spun on one toe like a ballet dancer; though he had never even seen a ballet dancer. His one foot was free and the sharp toe of his riding-boot bit with savage cruelty into Lemmy Macklein's shin. Lemmy gave a cry of agony and staggered. His gun swung upwards. Duke grabbed his wrist, twisted. The gun clattered to the floor. Duke's balled fist rammed into Lemmy's waistline. The lean saloon-keeper doubled, was straightened up again by a blow to the chin. This time he went all the way, landed on his back, lay still. After the crash there was a petrified silence. This was the first time anybody had seen the great Lemmy slugged in his own bar-room.

With his gun in one hand, his belt slung over his other arm, Duke faced the room. It was then that another diversion occurred. The batwings swung and Sheriff Sam Brighouse entered the place.

'What's going on here?'

Duke smiled a little: everybody seemed to be asking that question tonight. The sheriff came further into the place. The sick-looking gunfighter Kid Stone was behind him. Duke wondered where the two of them had been all this time.

A man spoke up: Duke recognized one of Lemmy's lap-dogs. 'This fancy gink started to wreck the joint. He pulled a gun on Lemmy an' Mose.'

Mose, climbing to his feet now, gave his feeble backing then quailed as Duke turned on him.

'Put that gun away, Duke,' said Sheriff

Brighouse. He was sober now and seemed to be carrying a chip on his shoulder. With one of the fastest gunmen in the West at his elbow – well, what could he lose?

'Don't I get a chance to speak my piece, too?' Duke almost snarled. He was getting tired of being told what to do.

Kid Stone moved to the sheriff's side now and stood facing Duke, negligently. But there was a subtle challenge about his attitude, too. There was always something a little challenging about the Kid's attitudes.

Duke slid his gun into its holster and began to fit the gun-belt around his lean waist. He had been pushed far enough. If Kid Stone wanted to make a grandstand play – well, he was ready for him. Duke was pretty fast himself, but, never having seen the Kid in action, he wasn't sure whether he could take him or not. The Kid had the reputation of being very fast. He had killed lots of folks who tried to haze him. It was best for a man to leave him alone. Still, if a man stopped to think those kind of thoughts maybe he lived longer – but felt lower than a snake's belly most of the time.

The atmosphere was electric. When the batwings were swung roughly open again it was as if a bomb had been dropped. But the tension was broken.

Two men came in.

'We want you, sheriff,' said Ron Purcell.

Sam Brighouse was persuaded against putting Duke in jail. But he insisted that the dapper little fighting-cock ride back to the ranch with him in the morning, where he (the sheriff) would investigate the murder of Hank Butler in Mud Hollow. Duke said he hoped folks wouldn't think he was running away. It was pointed out to him that he had already amply proven to everybody – most of all to Lemmy Macklein and his boy, Mose – that he wasn't the kind who ran away from anything.

Kid Stone elected to ride with the sheriff and Duke, so Charlie Pinto went along also to kind of balance things. Doc Logan said Pete Manetti wasn't fit enough to ride, so Ron Purcell stayed behind in town to kind of keep an eye on the lean waddy who was liable to break out of the clinic and try to shoot the place up in an attempt to find the hombre who slugged him.

At the last moment it was decided to take Walt Crisp's body back to the ranch, too: Ron Purcell figured the Old Man would be mighty peeved if this wasn't done. So a buckboard was hired and the blanket-shrouded form loaded upon it.

Ron watched the little cavalcade until it disappeared into the rising sun, then he turned back to town. Maybe he would be able to do a little quiet investigating on his ownsome now. He hadn't been the Cattlemen's Association's youngest troubleshooter years ago for nothing. . . .

Pete Manetti had given his word that he would rest up that morning. Pete was an ornery cuss, as dangerous as a diamond-backed sidewinder. But he kept his promises. Even that, however, was not all to the good, for Pete had sworn that when he learned the identity of the one who had slugged him he would perforate the skunk as full of holes as a sieve. Ron knew Pete would keep that promise, too, if he could.

There would be more bloody murder.

Ron had seen so much of it during his comparatively short life. Compared with some of the burgs he had known, Rampage, despite its bloodcurdling title, had been a fairly peacable place. Until yesterday! The murder of old Hank Butler seemed to have unleashed some cruel and malignant force; and Ron had a creepy feeling that that force was yet far from spent.

He could not help feeling also that the deaths of Hank Butler and Walt Crisp, the bushwhack attempt outside Lemmy's Place, the slugging of Pete Manetti, were all tied in together. The rustling could be tied in somewhere, too. Hell, it must be! The thought that all the crimes, or even one or two of them, were separate ones didn't bear thinking about – it was too crazy.

Maybe Walt Crisp had known something. Maybe, if he had lived he would have been able to put a finger on the man who murdered his partner, Hank. . . . The killer must belong to Rampage – or even to the Loop V. Ron wondered what the Old Man would have to say about this last theory.

While he was pondering, Ron's steps led him almost automatically to the town's one and only Commercial Hotel. He had to work pretty fast, for if he didn't get back to Doc Logan's place by lunchtime Pete Manetti was liable to bust loose.

Ron went through the hotel doors with a loping swing, almost skittling the person who happened to be coming out at the same time.

Indignant brown eyes blazed into his. He fumbled his hat off, almost dropped it.

'I beg your pardon, ma'am,' he said. 'I guess I wasn't looking where I was goin'.'

The storm-clouds cleared a little; he looked so truly contrite. 'I guess you weren't,' she said.

'I hope I haven't hurt you, ma'am.'

She dimpled. 'No.'

She turned away from him, began to descend the steps. He could not resist throwing a surreptitious glance after her. Her figure was trim, comely, only just short of voluptuous. Her hips swayed in tight, modish riding-breeches. Her shoulders were broad in a white shirtwaist with a well-worn leather vest of fancy Mexican design. Her hair, cascading from beneath a mannish and battered Stetson, was dark, with chestnut glints as the morning sunlight caught it.

The doors closed between them. Ron crossed to the desk.

The clerk was a thin, shifty-looking character with a prominent adam's apple. A lickspittling little counter-jumper, he was now in his own domain and would take advantage of the fact. He wasn't the kind to give out information willingly.

Ron glanced quickly around. There was nobody else in the lobby. He bellied up to the desk. The clerk straightened himself but could not reach the cowboy's height. He looked up enquiringly, shiftily.

'Mornin',' said Ron affably.

'Morning.' The clerk added 'sir', then looked like he wished he hadn't. Why should he be civil to this saddletramp, who, surely, was not a prospective guest?

The cowboy reached out with one long arm, grabbed the register, twisted it around. He leaned his elbow on the desk, ignoring the clerk now, and began to run his finger down the signatures in the book.

The clerk let out an explosively indignant breath. 'Ex-cuse me!' He grabbed hold of the top of the book.

A brown fist which felt like a cannonball descended with crashing force on his wrist. He yelped, backed, nursing the injured member. He found himself gazing into a pair of eyes like hot steel in the grim scarred face of the cow puncher. He lowered his own eyes and saw then that the scar-faced young man with the killer's eyes now had a couple of dollar bills between two fingers of one hand.

The young man raised his other hand, balled it into a fist once more. 'Which'll you have – this, or this?'

The clerk looked wildly about him. The cowboy did not seem to move but the muzzle of a gun suddenly appeared over the edge of the desk.

'*Or this?*'

The gun muzzle disappeared. Only then could the clerk bring himself to reach out quivering fingers and grab the money as if it was the last thing between him and eternity – as indeed it might well have been.

CHAPTER VI

'I want to know what new visitors you've had in during the last coupla weeks.'

'L-let me look, sir.' The clerk twisted the ledger around and scanned it with a great show of concentration. Eventually, he said, 'Just half-a-dozen, sir, and one of them has already gone again.'

'Which one is that?'

The clerk twisted the book again, stabbed a finger.

'Septimus B. Jones. I-I wouldn't actually call him a new visitor though, sir. He's a travelling salesman – travels in – er – hum – ladies undergarments I believe, sir. He's been coming here off and on for the last six months or so. Last time he was only here a couple of days.'

'When did he leave?'

'Yesterday, sir. Yesterday morning on the early stage.'

'Hum,' said Ron Purcell. 'I take it the other five people you mentioned are still here.'

'Yes, sir. The three cattle-buyers, sir . . .'

'Three?' Ron remembered Kid Stone had mentioned cattle-buyers, but only two of them.

'Yes, sir.' The clerk stabbed a finger again, grinned weakly. 'Messrs Spingle, Crane and Dobbs.'

Ron wondered what Spingle had been doing alone while Crane and Dobbs fronted for him in town. Or what Crane had been doing while . . . or what Dobbs had been doing . . .

He let it go. 'And the other two?'

'A Mr Jeff Laing, rancher, and his daughter, Maria.'

The cowboy's eyebrows rose. 'Jeff Laing! And was that Miss Maria I almost ran into when I was coming in here?'

'Er – yes, sir.'

'Hum,' said Ron again. He wondered what old mossy-back Jeff of Montana was doing in this neck of the woods. And with his daughter as his only companion, too.

His hand shot out, grabbed a handful of the clerk's none too clean shirt-front. The man gulped, looked like he was about to faint.

'I ain't asked you anything y'understand?' said this terrible scarfaced cowhand.

'N-no, sir. Of course not, sir.'

'D'you know where Messrs Spingle, Crane an' Dobbs are now?'

'All three went out about a half-hour ago. I don't know where they went, sir.'

'I may be wanting a room here a little later. D'yuh think you can fix that for me?' Ron let the man go.

'Why – why, yes, sir. C-certainly, sir.'

'You an' me are gonna be friends,' said the cowboy, suddenly amiable. Despite the terrible scar, he was quite handsome when he smiled.

'So-long,' he said.

'S-so-long, sir.'

The clerk watched the broad shoulders, the swaying horseman's walk, the way the hands swung at the hips, the right one almost brushing the scarred walnut butt of the Colt in its tied-down holster. The door swung to behind this killer and the clerk breathed a sigh of relief.

Ron walked down the street and went into a small saloon called The Buggy. In size and layout, this place was, in some folks' eyes, inferior to The Golden Lizard. But it had been up far longer and had its staunch adherents in the old townsfolk and other people who wanted a drink, a chat, a game, without being pestered by loud music and loudmouthed percentage girls. There were also quite a few people who did not hold with the way Lemmy ran things, although they did not run around shouting the fact – there were too many of Lemmy's sycophants and toughs in the town.

The place was kept by a large mild-mannered character called Tombstone Mike. Deceptively mild-mannered, but when roused a raging madman. He was a particular friend of Ron Purcell's, having known the youngster in his troubleshooting days.

Ron was pleased to find that, being early, the place was empty except for Mike polishing glasses behind the small zinc-lined bar. Mike crowed with pleasure, hooked a bottle of best whiskey from down below somewhere, skidded it across the bar, together with a glass.

'Thought you were dead, yuh young polecat,' he said insultingly.

Ron grinned, poured himself a drink and did not speak until he had downed it. Then he asked about the three strangers, Spingle, Crane and Dobbs.

'The cattle-buyers,' said Mike. 'Funny you should mention them. They've bin in here every morning for a drink since they hit town.'

'Have you seen 'em this morning yet?'

'Nope.' Mike drew a wet finger across the bar. 'What are you smelling after, Ron? Or don't you want to talk about it?'

'Let me ask you another question first.'

'Go ahead.'

'D'yuu know a little drummer called Septimus B. Jones who visits town every now and then?'

'Cain't say I do. Last drummer I had in here was months ago. He was a lanky guy named Peters who tried to sell me a pair of fancy suspenders. You can't miss them drummers – they suttinly stay in there slugging. Maybe this Jones character used Lemmy's Place.'

'Maybe he don't drink,' said Ron. 'D'yuh know somep'n, Mike?'

'What?'

'Jeff Laing's in town. You remember Jeff don't you, Mike?'

'Do I remember Jeff? I'll say! What's he doing here?'

'Search me. He's got his daughter, Maria, with him.'

'Yeh, I remember the gel. She was just a nipper when I saw her last . . .'

Ron smiled faintly. 'She's no nipper now.'

'Say, Ron, d'yuh remember the time when . . .' Mike broke off, caught hold of his companion's wrist. 'Here are our three friends, the cattle-buyers.'

Ron raised his head a little, saw the three men through the mirror above the bar. They were all big, hard-looking. Hard; cattle-buyers got to be that way: with some of the hardbitten old ranchers with whom they dealt they had to be that way.

They bellied against the bar. The elder one, redfaced, running to fat said 'Howdy'. The second eldest grunted. The younger, who would be about Ron's age, didn't say a thing. The elder called for drinks, including Ron and Mike. Ron called cheers; no names were exchanged. They were a tough-looking trio all right; and the youngest, at least, was in the pink of condition; muscles rippled beneath his shirt when he moved. He was sullen, looked like a nasty customer to rouse; the type who was easily roused, too, by the look of him.

He glanced at Ron sullenly from under heavy eyelids. His face was not unhandsome; but a little lumpy, a little lopsided. Despite his comparative youth, he looked like a man who had fought in the prize-ring; or maybe just around the camps and ranches for purses put up by the boys, with plenty of side bets.

Ron wondered which was Mister Spingle, which Crane, which Dobbs. They looked more like a trio of road-agents – or, maybe, rustlers! – than cattle-buyers. Ron almost laughed out loud, knowing full well that in the lawless West, only tenderfeet – who didn't know any better anyway – judged folks by their appearances. The most cold-blooded thief and killer Ron had ever known had looked like a saint, and, when the vigilantes hanged him, women wept for his blue eyes and curly, golden locks.

Ron called for drinks all round. The younger cattle-buyer opened his sullen mouth as if to say something, then closed it again soundlessly. They took their drinks, toasted each other once more without wasting words. Then, as quickly and almost as silently as they had come, the cattle-buyers left. Still no introductions had been made and in this lawless place one man did not ask another man who he was . . . The batwings swung gently in the sunshine . . . 'Are they always like that?' asked Ron.

'The young one, yes,' said Mike. 'But the other two are usually more affable.'

'Maybe they been to see the Old Man,' grinned Ron. 'The Old Man does kind of have that effect on people.'

'Yuh durn' tootin',' exploded Mike.

'Wal, you should know, if anybody does,' said Ron. 'You've known him a damsight longer'n I have. An' you used to work for him didn't you?'

Ron, on the basis of never asking awkward questions, had never directly before mentioned Mike's association with the Old Man. It was something that Mike had never seemed keen on talking about. Now, as he watched his old friend's face sober, Ron wished he had kept his mouth shut.

But finally Mike said: 'I can remember the Old Man coming here. Like I told you before when we first met again in this neck o' the woods, I came down here after the blood-bath at the Panhandle. I was sick of troubleshooting – killing. It was pretty peaceful down here then. A few little spreads, a little clapboard and tent settlement. The Injuns had long since been driven away, people were planning, working, building a new life for themselves . . .'

Mike stared away at the batwings as if he waited for some great revelation at their opening. But they did not open, and Ron Purcell knew that his old friend was not seeing them anyway; what he saw was half-obscured by the mists of time, so near and yet so far, every man's memory of what might have been.

It was as if Mike was talking to himself . . . 'I had hopes of starting a little place like this, of diggin' myself a groove to settle in at last – but I hadn't yet got enough dinero, so I went to work as a cowhand. The biggest spread then was old Pop Game's place. You could have put it in one corner of the Loop V as it is now, but in them days it was the biggest, bein' almost twice as big as most of its neighbours. Old Pop was a likeable ol' cuss an' he thought all the world of his ranch. He couldn't afford to pay a helluva lot, but his boys – there wuz only six of us – were his family. He was a childless widower, had no other family. We had our own bunkhouse, as was right an' proper, but were allus welcome in the ranchhouse on our off-times . . .'

Mike paused, filled two glasses from the depleted

bottle of whiskey, pushed one across to Ron. The younger man acknowledged with a gesture, did not break the thread of things by speaking.

Mike went on: 'The Old Man rode in one day with three more riders. They rode into town, that is. One of the men got into an argument with a storekeeper an' shot him dead. I disremember the storekeeper's name now, but he was a harmless enough cuss, an' suttinly not a professional gun slinger like the one who killed him. It was the first killing they'd had in town since the old massacre which gave it its name. They had no law – nobody really knew what to do. The strangers, particularly the eldest one – an' you know who that was – said their friend had been provoked.'

'They produced a couple of witnesses, both of whom could've been got with a few free drinks – but they stuck to their story. The storekeeper hadn't been anybody very important. Everybody was pretty busy minding their own business, earning a living for themselves. Finally the affair blew over, was forgotten. The Old Man and his two pardners – right now I don't even remember their names – stayed on in town. They seemed to be minding their own business too, as if they were ashamed of having stepped off on the wrong foot in the first place. They seemed to have plenty of money, and they were pretty generous with it. In some quarters they became very popular. Me, I knew lobo wolves when I saw 'em, I could take 'em, or I could leave 'em . . .'

Mike paused. Then went on again, reflectively. 'It's a funny thing. The two men who acted as witnesses for the Old Man and his friends after the killing – they left the territory an' never came back. They hadn't been much credit to the place and I guess nobody missed 'em – except me, who, bein' an old law-dog, had suspicioning and noticing things plumb trained into me. The Old Man and his three hardcases began to get a little clique of followers around them. The town was growing – more and more permanent buildings were going up. The ranches were growing – there was work for all kinds of people an' all kinds of people began to move in. The rougher sort always seemed to gravitate eventually to the Old Man. Then the Old Man – he seemed like an old lobo wolf even in those days – began to build his ranch.'

Mike paused again. Ron Purcell said nothing, waited. Seemed like he had heard it all before – or something a lot like it. He knew what was coming. But he waited for it to be told.

And, finally, the old lawman went on. He seemed to echo the younger man's thoughts as he said, 'The rest is pretty much ancient history. It happened then and its still happening. As long as men are eaten up with greed it'll keep happening. So I guess it'll keep on to eternity, the strong gobbling up the weak . . .'

Ron Purcell was a little surprised. He had never heard his rather taciturn old friend wax so eloquent before. Mike was quite a dark horse, an educated one, at that – Ron hadn't known the old mossy-horn had it in him.

'The Old Man got himself a big stock of prime

beef, the best that had ever been seen in this territory. He'd already got himself a big stock of troubleshooters. Their hangout up till then had been Rampage's first saloon, a clapboard place owned by an unpleasant character, a half-breed called Chino Tommy. They moved from there to the big new bunkhouse at the Loop V . . .'

'I know it,' said Ron with a faint smile. 'I've got to hand it to the Old Man, that's the best bunkhouse I've ever seen.'

'The Old Man did allus look after his boys pretty well,' said Mike. 'You can't blame them for sticking to him . . . Still, to get back to Chino Tommy's place.' Mike grinned sardonically. 'It's the last we'll hear of it – just after the Old Man's boys moved out, it was burned to the ground, and Chino Tommy was burned with it. There wasn't much left of anything, including Tommy. Funny thing was, he was the only one there at the time – it was almost as if everybody else had had prior warning.

'Still, maybe I'm romancing.' Tommy's loss was my gain, anyway. I moved in, built my own place. For some time I owned the only saloon in Rampage an' everybody came here – even the Old Man and his boys. For some time I was too busy to take much notice of what was happening out on the range. By the time I sat up an' took notice – not that it was any of my business anyway – the Old Man had bought everybody out. He offered good prices. He was very persuasive too. Although there were no actual killings there were nasty rumours about beatings, burnings and suchlike.

'I rode out to see my old boss, Pop Game, but he had already left and two Loop V boys were sort of caretaking the place. They resented my visit. They tried to push me an' there was a fight. They were pretty tough, but I guess they didn't know any of the tricks – they picked on a harmless saloonkeeper and he turned into a curly wolf. It was like taking candy from kids. I am afraid I vented all my spleen on those two bozos.' Mike's voice was sober. 'I crippled one of them. That was when I fell out of favour with the Loop V.'

'I wonder you didn't tell me all this when I first landed in this territory, Mike,' said Ron.

'I didn't want to try an' influence you, son. Knowing you, I figured you'd rather make your own decisions. Hell, what's the harm in working for the Loop V anyway? The Old Man's a law-abiding citizen now – a mighty important one. Not that he ever did step right outside the law, he was too clever for that. We had law in Rampage eventually but it couldn't touch the Old Man. And what he had done before he came to Rampage, who he was, where he came from nobody ever found out. The name he used might've been his real one and it might not've. In any case, pretty soon everybody began to call him the Old Man; and they forgot he'd ever been called anything else.'

'Did the Loop V ever try to push you out?' asked Ron Purcell.

'Wal, no, strangely enough, they didn't. They uttered some pretty dark threats after I beat up two of their boys, but I guess the Old Man never gave the final word. Maybe he figured I wasn't important enough to bother with. I was still the only saloon-keeper in Rampage. Lemmy Macklein didn't turn up till some time later . . .'

'What happened then?'

'Nothin' really. Folks said at first that Lemmy was in cahoots with the Old Man, but I never found anything to support this theory. They seemed to leave each other severely alone. The Old Man had what he wanted out on the range; I guess he figured the town could go to hell in its own way as long as that didn't interfere in any way with him and his boys.'

'Were there a lot of killings in those early days?'

'Not so many as you might have expected. Funny thing – the only important killing I can remember was that of three of the Loop V's own men: the three, strangely enough, who had rode in with the Old Man in the first place. They were drygulched, shot in the back on a dark trail one night. They had their wages with 'em, they were robbed, nobody was ever pulled in for it. Folks forget 'em. The only one I remember was the eldest, a big middle-aged gink called Straker, who was the fastest thing with a gun that I have ever seen in my life. Faster than you, I think, son. Faster maybe than our old friend, now among us once more, Kid Stone . . .'

Mike paused. And when he spoke again his voice had grown weary. 'Hell, it was all a long time ago. I'm gettin' old, Ron. When you get to my age you figure there are some things you'd best forget. Let's have another drink.'

They had another drink and after that Ron left. He had plenty to think about, though none of it really concerned him now, had anything to do with the job in hand. The sight of Maria Laing crossing the street before him diverted him a little. She did not see him. Why should she? He realized suddenly that it was noon and hastened towards Doc Logan's place.

CHAPTER VII

Mrs Logan met him on the front stoop. She looked a little flurried. 'Have you seen your friend, that Pete?' she asked.

'No.' Ron silently cursed himself. Why hadn't he got back here sooner? 'Where's the doc?' he asked.

'He's out on a case. He went in to see your friend first and said he seemed quite contented. But I went through the back just to take him some coffee and he wasn't there. I've looked all around. He's vanished.'

Ron put in some silent cursing against Pete. The cunning skunk must have slipped out as soon as the doc had left. Ron couldn't help feeling it was a filthy trick to play on the old lady, who was looking really worried. He followed her into the house, through to the back. The window of the bedroom was half-open. The same window had let in the killer of old Walt Crisp; and now it had provided an escape-hatch for the truculent Pete Manetti, complete with man-sized chip on shoulder.

Ron wondered if Pete had taken his gun. He soon

discovered that the lean troubleshooter had done just that; he'd be as deadly as a killer-bronc with a burr under its tail.

Ron made a circuit of the house. Maybe something had happened to Pete – though he couldn't imagine anybody being able to take Pete unawares the way Walt Crisp had been taken: Pete hadn't been that sick. Ron finished up by cursing the lean waddy once more. What a bunch of jackasses to be saddled with! First Duke went on the prod; and now, if Ron didn't miss his guess, Pete was following the little dude's horrible example. And it wasn't funny either: Pete was a lot less even-tempered and good-natured that Duke. Ron went back through the house, told Mrs Logan he was going to look for Manetti. He told her not to worry. Then he left.

He made the rounds of the eating houses, saloons and other places of that kind. He gave the bawdy-houses a miss because he knew Pete was a confirmed woman-hater. He called on Mike again and on the rat-faced clerk at the commercial hotel.

Nobody had seen hide or hair of Pete Manetti. Ron wondered if the lean ranny had taken it into his head to ride back to the ranch. Then he remembered that Pete's horse was still hitched in the small barn beside the doctor's place, and this fact suddenly began to assume a new and terrible significance.

Ron had assumed that Pete would walk the short step to the centre of town, not wanting to risk giving the game away to Mrs Logan by leading the horse out. But what if he hadn't walked at all, what if he had indeed been surprised, taken away. Nothing seemed too fantastic now.

Ron wasn't sure what to do next. His steps led him, almost automatically, towards Lemmy's Place. He had been in once before to ask questions, but without success. Maybe Pete and him had been chasing each other's tails without knowing it.

The sun was brilliant. To avoid the glare he moved into the shadows of the boardwalk. This manouvre brought him near the window of the all-purpose emporium next to Lemmy's Place. Something in its cluttered window caught his eye and he stopped dead.

During the recent terrible press of events he had forgotten the battered black sombrero he had found out in the badlands. The only clue yet – if it was a clue – in this whole tangled mess. Now the significance of the hat was brought back to him with redoubled force.

He got nearer to the window, almost pressed his nose to it. He wanted to make perfectly sure.

There was only one sombrero in the window. It had pride of place, elevated on a stand above a clutter of fancy belts and holsters, sheath-knives, bandannas, boxes of cartridges, chaps, riatas, quirts and other appurtenances of purely Western civilization. It was a real dandy of a hat, soft, rich black felt. Its brim was unusually wide, even for a Mexican style sombrero, and had a flamboyant curl. Its lizard-skin band was broad, ornate.

It wasn't the kind of hat Ron Purcell would have worn, particularly with the duds he sported now. But he had to admit there was something fascinating, richly flamboyant, about that black hat. A little man would look silly in it. It would take a big man, a handsome man preferably, to take it off. Ron himself could have worn it. So could Kid Stone, who had a flair for dress. There were others, but Ron couldn't think of them offhand.

The sight of the hat had sent all kinds of new thoughts spinning through his head. But he didn't aim to go off half-cocked all over the places, thinking he'd solved everything. The first thing to do was to make sure this hat was, indeed, exactly the same as the one he had found in the badlands after his discovery of the Mud Hollow murder and the cattle-rustling.

He had almost forgotten Pete Manetti. That hornery cuss could wait anyway: he was quite big enough to look after himself.

Ron turned back, made his way to the stables. He took the battered black sombrero from his saddle-bag. Kind of a silly place to leave evidence, anyway, now he came to think about it. He tucked it out of sight in his shirt.

He retraced his steps to the emporium window. He looked around him before surreptitiously bringing his find out to the light of day.

The two hats were the same all right, except for the fact that the battered one Ron held was a mite larger than the one in the window. Rod hid his clue once more and entered the shop.

The little storekeeper scuttled from the shadows in the back. 'I'd like to try on a sombrero like that black one you have in the window,' said Ron brusquely. He had never asked for anything quite as fancy as that before. He could just imagine what Duke Linstone would say had he been there. Ron repeatedly joshed the little cowpoke for his flamboyant taste in apparel.

'That's the only one I've got, suh,' gabbled the little man. 'I had two from a drummer, just to try 'em out. I sold the other one as soon as I got 'em in.'

You didn't have to ask this galoot for information, he flung it at you. For free, at that. 'I ain't seen one in the window before,' said Ron. 'When did you get 'em in?'

'Coupla days ago.'

'I ain't seen anybody sporting one around town. Who did you sell the other to?'

The storekeeper didn't seem to think all these questions were out of place. He seemed only too glad to answer them. He wrinkled his brow, snapped his fingers.

'I know the fellah well by sight – jest cain't remember his name.'

'Does he live in town?'

'I think so.' A great light broke upon the little man's countenance . . . 'Yeh, I remember who it was now! Jacko Chubbs. Jacko likes purty things.'

Ron Purcell's heart sank. He realized he had been building too much on the storeman's answers to his questions. Jacko Chubbs was the town fool, a shambling odd-job man who couldn't do even the simplest jobs properly. He had a weakness for squandering his cash occasionally on something luxurious with which to embellish his rags. A gaudy kerchief, an ornate belt, a polka-dot shirt, a new hat . . .

The storeman had vanished, could be heard rooting around in the window. He reappeared, holding the black sombrero before him as if he was bearing a crown on a cushion of velvet.

'If you would like to step in the back, suh, I have a mirror.'

Feeling a little foolish, Ron followed him.

He tried the hat in front of the long opera-glass and was relieved to find that it was too big for him.

The garrulous storekeeper said, 'I kin get another one for you, huh.' He hesitated. 'Though it may take a little time. I got these from Mr Jones who – er – um – usually supplies me with ladies' undergarments. This was a new line he had picked up – just samples. He left two with me to try them out.'

So Septimus B. Jones was cropping up again was he? 'How often does Mr Jones call on you?' asked Ron.

'At irregular intervals, suh. Seldom less than a month between them though, suh. He travels extensively. A very jolly gentleman and a good salesman.'

And was that all? wondered Ron. He looked at the hat dubiously. 'Now I've seen it on me, I'm not so keen on one as I was.'

The storeman was a salesman, too. He took the sombrero gently from Ron's hands, but eyed the cowboy's battered Stetson with disfavour.

'I have just the thing for you, suh. If you will wait one moment.'

He bustled away, only to return a few seconds later with a dove-grey Stetson with a plain black leather band. Ron tried it on. It fit him perfectly and he had to admit it was a right handsome hat. He bought it. The shopkeeper put it in a big bag for him.

He was passing through the door of the emporium into the afternoon sunshine when he heard the shots. They came from the direction of Lemmy's Place.

He changed the bag from his left hand to his right as he ran, awkwardly in his high-heeled riding boots. He slowed down when he reached the batwings, pushed them open. He passed through them then stopped dead, leaving them swinging gently behind him.

He took in the tableau in one sweeping glance.

There weren't many people in the place. Just a few spread around the walls out of harm's way. And the three others near the bar. Two standing, one lying down on the floor.

The one on the floor was Pete Manetti and Ron knew, by the horrible sprawl of the body, that Pete was dead. Ron made an almost instinctive movement, then froze as Kid Stone's voice rapped out.

'Hold it, my friend.'

Ron spread his arms a little, the hatbag still dangling in the left one. He eyed Stone and his employer, Lemmy Macklein.

Lemmy was leaning against the bar. His face, apart from the bruises Duke Linstone had imprinted on it, was very pale. Kid stood at the side of him, but a little nearer to the body. In Kid's fist was the inevitable gun, pointed in an almost negligent fashion at Ron Purcell.

'What happened?' asked the newcomer flatly.

The Kid's voice was mild. 'He was a pardner o' yourn, so you've got a right to know. He came blustering in here half drunk an' accused Lemmy of having him beat up an' worse things. He kept shouting so Lemmy couldn't argue with him. He wouldn't properly explain what kind of a bee he had in his bonnet. Finally he called Lemmy out. Lemmy was gonna try an' take him. But he would've been throwing his life away – I knew he had a twisted wrist from that shindig he had with your other pardner last night. So I stepped in the breach . . .' Kid finished with a little shrug, a gesture towards the recumbent form almost at his feet.

Ron felt as if somebody had kicked him in the guts. He had no doubt that the gunman had told the truth. Whatever else Kid Stone might be, he wasn't a liar. He wondered if Pete had had any grounds for his allegations against Lemmy Macklein. Who could tell with a hothead like Pete. Nobody would ever know now.

A fine job he had made of looking after the lean waddy. If he hadn't wasted his time chasing hats he might have been able to prevent this.

Kid Stone said, 'It was like I said, Ron. It was a fair fight. I beat him to the draw.'

He looked around him. Other men nodded their heads, murmured assent. Lemmy Macklein said: 'I was gonna try an' take him.' He held up his right hand limply. Around the wrist was a new white bandage. 'If the Kid hadn't stepped in I'd be a dead duck now.'

'All right, Kid,' said Ron Purcell, almost wearily.

'You can put your gun away.'

Kid Stone smiled thinly, holstered his weapon. Ron Purcell began to move forward. Other folks, peering, began to come through the batwings behind him.

Ron said: 'I thought you were at the Loop V, Kid.'

'I came back right away, leaving the sheriff. I didn't like the company there.'

No doubt the Old Man had in some way antagonized the pale-faced gunfighter, reflected Ron. He bent over what was left of Pete Manetti. Two heavy slugs had made a mess of the lean chest.

He straightened up. 'I'll go get his horse,' he said. There didn't seem much else he could do.

Kid Stone came a little nearer. He spoke softly. Probably nobody else heard him. 'I'm sorry, Ron. I knew he was a pard of yours an' I didn't want to cut him down. But I couldn't stand by an' let him shoot Lemmy to ribbons.'

Ron said nothing. What could he say? The Kid sounded truly contrite: he was a damnably queer mixture of a man. Ron turned away from him, passed through the batwings.

He went along to Doc Logan's place and got Pete's horse. The little doctor had arrived back home. Ron took him aside, quietly told him what had happened. But there was nothing Doc Logan could do for Pete now.

Ron took the horse back to Lemmy's place. One of the barmen helped him to carry Pete's body out and tie it to the saddle. Then Ron went and fetched his own horse from the stable. Lemmy Macklein and

Kid Stone had reappeared again. The latter asked:

'Are you taking him back to the ranch?'

'Yeh.'

'You'll probably meet the sheriff there or on the trail. Tell him that, if he wants me, I'll be right here.'

'An' there'll be plenty of witnesses, too,' added Lemmy Macklein drily.

'I'll bet there will,' said Ron Purcell, then wondered if he was being unfair. All the people who had backed the Kid's self-defence plea inside the saloon had not been Lemmy's boys: Ron had noticed a few reliable townsfolk among them.

The only thing he could ponder on now was whether Pete Manetti had been justified in his allegations against the saloon-owner. Had Lemmy had the lean cowpoke beaten up? And, if so – why?

He mounted his own horse and led the other one with its grim burden. Down the main drag of Rampage, out on to the range.

Pete's horse was a little jittery and he had to pause and gentle it from time to time. His heart was heavy as he glanced at the grim burden in the saddle, lashed there like a side of beef. This was what was left of the man he had stayed behind to protect.

It was little consolation to him to reflect that Pete had not actually kept his word or, at least, had hightailed it from Doc Logan's place as soon as noon struck.

He had run bullheaded into his own death.

Ron glanced down at his saddlebag. In there reposed the hat he had bought. If he had not wasted time shopping and asking fool questions he might've saved Pete's life, even if it meant standing up against Kid Stone in order to do so.

And what good had he done by his shopping expedition anyway? The only fancy black sombrero sold in Rampage had been purchased by the town fool, Jacko Chubbs.

Ron didn't know Jacko very well. Maybe Jacko wasn't quite such a fool as he pretended to be. . . !

Ron pulled himself up short, cursed himself silently. What was he: a detective gone haywire? You couldn't fight everything with your wits. This was violence and sudden death. He had seen much of it before and could not turn his face away from it now. His wits were needed – but, no matter how he might try to stifle the thought, his guns and fists were needed too, the way they had been needed – and used! – so many times before.

He bore the gunfighter's brand and maybe nothing would wash it off – until he finished up like poor Pete, lolling there beside him.

The afternoon sunshine was very bright, garishly mocking him. Out of it rode a black figure which, shading his eyes against the glare, Ron presently recognized as Sheriff Brighouse.

A few seconds later the lawman reined in his horse, his glance passing from Ron to the saddle contents of the other horse.

'Pete Manetti!'

'Yeh.' Tersely, Ron told his story.

The sheriff had little to say. His face puckered with worry, he said, 'I'll see the Kid as soon as I get back to town.'

Ron asked: 'What made the Kid leave the Loop V so quickly?'

'The Old Man asked if the Kid was a deputy of mine. I had to admit that he wasn't – leastways, not officially. The Old Man said that, as this was official business the Kid had no right there. The Kid didn't say anything – he just walked out.'

'An' rode right back to town an' shot one of the Old Man's boys.'

'It was self-defence you said, Ron.'

'That's what everybody said.' The cowboy's voice sounded almost as weary as the lawman's.

The latter said, 'I guess it's best for Pete to be taken to the ranch. But I hope the Old Man don't start blaming everybody before he knows the facts of the case.'

'I won't push him, if that's what you mean. We don't want any more wild killings.'

The sheriff nodded. They parted, went their separate ways.

CHAPTER VIII

The Old Man stood on his veranda watching the two horses come slowly towards him. One with a rider upright in the saddle, the other with something sack-like slung across its back, lashed there like so much beef, bobbing with a see-saw motion as the beast's hooves thudded on the uneven sun-baked ground.

Like some bird of prey he was standing there motionless, Ron Purcell reflected. Had it been any lesser man one might have thought he was literally stunned by shock – as well he might be. In the matter of hours, two of his men had been brought in hanging face downwards across their saddles. And only a short time ago he had returned from burying a third!

Things like that just did not happen to the Old Man. He had once *made* such things happen, but that was long ago, and for many years there had been peace and plenty. Even Ron Purcell – troubleshooter, whose memories of violence and sudden death were much clearer – had to admit there was an element of fantasy about it all.

He reined in the two horses before the Old Man, who leaned on his stick, looking down at him piercingly.

'Pete Manetti?' The voice was like the croak of a buzzard.

'Yeh,' said Ron Purcell, and once more told his story.

The Old Man stood immobile through the whole narrative, his eyes so hidden now beneath the white bushy brows that he might have gone to sleep leaning there on his stick.

'Self-defence you say,' he grunted presently.

'Like I said, I didn't see it,' said Ron. 'But Kid Stone had plenty of good witnesses, not all of them friends of his and Lemmy's, who backed him up in that.'

The Old Man nodded almost mildly. 'Unlash the body an' bring it up here,' he said.

Ron Purcell did as he was told, remembering the way he had done the same with the body of old Hank Butler, only yesterday. Once more he laid the body at the feet of his boss as if as a sacrificial offering.

The Old Man suddenly became convulsed with life. His pent-up rage spewed forth in a malignant tide. Ron had stayed behind to look after Peter and had failed in that, had failed terribly! Although Pete had always been quite capable of looking after himself and, in fact, resented interference, Ron still half-blamed himself for the lean ranny's death. However, he didn't intend to stand such screaming, insulting abuse from the Old Man, which already was going beyond the bounds of reason.

'Cut it!' he bawled into the red, twisted face. 'Are you stark crazy? Cut it, or by God, I won't be responsible for what might happen.'

The Old Man shut up. But his face still worked and suddenly he lashed out at Ron with his stick. The young cowhand caught the stick with his hand, but even through his gloves it stung. He wrenched the stick from the Old Man's grasp and flung it across the veranda; for a moment he saw red, he wanted to grab that scrawny screaming buzzard's throat and choke the life from it.

But he remembered in time that this was an old man and he stepped back a little, letting his hands fall limply to his sides.

The Old Man was silent now, breathing heavily, but half-crouching as if he contemplated springing at the cowboy.

'Watch yourself,' said Ron Purcell. 'For Pete's sake, watch yourself.'

Then the Old Man relaxed too. His face became a wrinkled mask, his eyes were hidden once more. When he spoke, his voice was a husky toneless whisper.

'Get that Kid Stone. Get him!'

'When it comes to killing, I make my own decisions,' said Ron and turned on his heels and left the veranda.

He led the two horses away. The Old Man did not call after him. He wondered if he would be given his time. Under other circumstances, he would've quit anyway – but now he figured he had a job to do. Even if there was nothing he could do about the death of Pete Manetti, there still remained the mystery of the Butler and Crisp murders. And Hank and Walt had been his friends, too.

Burt Cooley, the foreman, came to him in the stables. 'I couldn't help hearing a bit of what went on, Ron. Pete Manetti was it?'

'Yeh.'

'How did it happen?'

'I'd rather not go through it all again just yet, Burt,' said Ron wearily. 'No doubt the Old Man will have his own version to tell you pretty soon.'

Burt looked at him stolidly as if a little uncertain of just how to take this. But everything was taken suddenly out of his hands by the Old Man's voice screaming, 'Burt.'

When he was mad he always yelled for his foreman that way. Only a man of Burt's middle-aged, even-tempered, phlegmatic temperament would've been able to stand the Old Man's tantrums for any length of time.

Burt was a good foreman. He knew his job and his men respected him. The Old Man's abuse ran off him like water from a duck's back. The abuse did not seem to touch Burt somehow because it did not shatter his calm and, in the eyes of others, did not seem to degrade him like it would've degraded another man. Maybe this was because whenever the Old Man hired a new rider he always told the latter that Cooley was the best ramrod in the territory: and the new boy would do what Cooley said, or the boss would want to know the reason why.

As Ron Purcell watched Burt shamble away he

was reflecting that the middle-aged cowhand had been with the Old Man since the early days. He wondered whether Burt remembered the Old Man's arrival in Rampage or whether Burt had come after that. He wondered whether Burt had known the three men who had been the Old Man's pardners – two of which, as far as Ron Purcell was concerned anyway, might well have been nameless . . . And the third called Straker, 'one of the fastest things with a gun' that Tombstone Mike, troubleshooter turned saloon-keeper, had seen in his life . . .

Charles Pinto was nowhere around, but now his sidekick, the Indian boy called Happy, came from the gloom at the back of the stables. Ron wondered if he had heard what had been going on; but Happy's dark face wore its usual wide, white-teethed grin, so friendly yet giving nothing away, as inscrutable as the features of his people were supposed to be.

He took the horses and promised to feed them. Ron carried the saddles to the empty bunkhouse and parked them there, then went on to the kitchen.

Barney, the obese cook, grunted a greeting. If he had heard anything he evidently didn't intend to divulge the fact. He was inscrutable, too, as inscrutable as a fat white Chinese idol.

Ron hadn't seen Barney since they had the slight disagreement yesterday morning when Barney objected to being raked out of bed at an early hour. The cook had nothing to be disgruntled about; he had won the argument anyway. Ron had made do with rustlings, had allowed the fat man to climb, grunting and grumbling, back into his bunk again.

Then Ron had ridden out and found the body of old Hank Butler. That was when it had all started, barely sixty hours ago. It seemed like much longer than that!

Barney was a good cook and soon had a huge meal ready for Ron. Steak, peas, french fries, flapjacks and syrup; lots of strong, hot, sweet coffee. Barney went into his cubbyhole to finish his washing-up and left the cowboy to it.

About half an hour later, when Ron was settling back and rolling himself a quirly, Burt Cooley put in an appearance again.

'The Old Man wants you to go out to the South range an' help with that wiring job, Ron.'

'All right.'

Burt turned away. Only before leaving the place did he turn and say:

'Both Walt an' Pete will be buried early to-morrow mornin'. The Old Man wants everybody to be present.'

Nothing more. The door closed gently.

Ron finished his smoke and rose. He called 'So-long' to Barney and received a grunted reply. He made tracks for the stables and saddled a fresh horse, choosing to leave his own special mount to finish his bag of oats and his rest.

The grinning Happy bade him *adios*. Leading the horse across the yard Ron almost ran into the elderly man and the girl who were crossing on foot to the ranch-house.

Ron wondered what Jeff Laing and Maria were doing here. 'Howdy,' he said.

The smallish, portly old man whirled in his tracks.

'By all that's holy! Ron Purcell!'

'How are yuh, Jeff?' Ron gripped the proffered hand. Out of the corner of his eye, he gleefully noted that Maria looked a little confused. With that delicate flush on her face, she was prettier than ever.

Old Jeff's grip was as strong as ever as he swung the young man round to face the girl before letting go of his hand.

'You remember Maria, don't yuh, Ron?'

'Sure I do. But I don't think she remembers me.'

The girl had regained her poise. She dimpled. 'Mr Ron Purcell and I bumped into each other in town this morning. I didn't remember him and I'm pretty sure he didn't remember me either.'

'You're right,' admitted Ron ruefully. 'You were pretty young when I saw you last.'

'Yes, and you wouldn't be very old yourself either. I've heard Dad talk of you. I recognized your name as soon as he spoke it.'

Jeff had been watching this bye-play with a whimsical expression on his chubby face. Now he spoke up again. 'When Ron worked for me he was about sixteen. You'd be about eight or nine, Maria.'

Ron took the small brown hand that was held out to him. 'I'm sorry I didn't recognize you in town, Miss Maria.'

She laughed gently. 'Please don't apologize, Mr Purcell. You were in a kind of a hurry anyway.'

'You useter call each other Ron and Maria in the old days,' put in Jeff, slyly.

Neither of them seemed to have anything to say to that. Ron remembered the girl how she used to be, lanky, coltish, with pigtails. No wonder he hadn't recognized this trim vision as Maria Laing.

Jeff broke the rather strained silence by volunteering some information and asking a question, all at the same time. 'I arranged to meet your boss, Ron. I heard he had some cattle to sell. Is it good cattle, son?'

'All the Loop V stock is good,' said Ron quite truthfully.

Then he saw that Jeff was gazing past him and he turned his head. The Old Man, walking on his stick, was making his way towards them. Ron didn't want another altercation with the old buzzard in front of Jeff Laing and his daughter, so he said, 'I'd best be getting along. I hope I'll see you both again.'

'Sure thing,' said Jeff. 'If you're in town to-night ask for us at the commercial hotel.'

'I'll do that.' Ron doffed his hat to the girl and went on his way. Her faint, rather quizzical smile went with him.

Three-quarters of an hour later he reached the South Range, where a sizeable bunch of the Loop V personnel were restringing wire to stop straying dogies. Among them was Duke Linstone. Ron took the little dude aside and told him what had happened to his friend, Pete.

Duke was all for riding into town right then and calling out Kid Stone, but finally Ron made him see reason.

'I'm going into town tonight anyway,' pronounced Duke flatly. 'You comin' along?'

'Yeh, I'm comin' along.' Ron thought he'd better do so in any case, if only to try and prevent Duke from finishing up the same way as Pete. Also it would give him a chance to pay that visit to Jeff Laing and Maria.

Lemmy's place seemed to be even fuller than usual. The noise was indescribable. Blue smoke partially obscured faces, so that, followed by Ron Purcell, Duke Linstone had to peer at people before he could recognize them. He returned greetings absently. He did not see the man he was looking for.

They reached the bar. Duke called for drinks then, out of the corner of his mouth, asked the barman, 'Where's Lemmy?'

'I couldn't say, suh. I haven't seen him all evening.'

It was difficult to judge whether the man was lying or not. He had the poker face of his kind; of the best-trained ones of his kind, too: it was Lemmy Macklein's boast that he hired only the best, the professional in all things. Professional gunmen and bouncers, professional entertainers and musicians, professional girls. . . .

'How about Kid Stone?' asked Duke.

'Last I seen of him he was leaving the place with the sheriff.' The man smiled thinly as if the thought pleased him.

'Is he under arrest or somep'n?'

'I couldn't say, suh. Him and the sheriff seemed to be on quite good terms.' The man excused himself and moved away.

Ron and Duke had a few more drinks. They did not see either Kid Stone or Lemmy Macklein. Duke had simmered down again and finally said, 'This place is giving me a headache. Let's go over to Tombstone Mike's.'

'All right.' Ron Purcell led the way.

At Mike's they were greeted jovially by the usual regulars. Duke was soon dragged into a school of poker players, a game of which he was inordinately fond. Ron was left at the bar with Mike. He said to his old friend, 'I'm going over to the commercial hotel. If Duke should happen to leave here before I get back will you send a boy for me pronto?'

Mike, who had heard of the death of Pete and guessed the way the cards were stacked, promised to play along.

Duke had a pile of chips in front of him and did not see his pardner leave.

The ratfaced desk-clerk boggled when he saw the scarfaced killer approaching him once more. He was mighty relieved when Ron asked were the Laings at home. Yes, if the gentleman was Mr Purcell, would he please go up.

The clerk watched the lean killer climb the stairs, his gun bobbing at his hip. The clerk admired Miss Maria from afar. He wondered how this hard-looking young gunny could've gotten to know the Laings so soon when it was only yesterday that he'd asked about them at this very desk. The clerk sighed, turning back to his pigeon holes; he often wished he was a hard-case with a few notches on his guns: maybe folks would take more notice of him then.

The Laings received Ron in the larger of the two rooms they occupied, the one in which the sleeping arrangements were hidden behind the screen. Judging by the pleasantly subtle perfume that hung over the place, Ron figured this must be the girl's room. He removed his hat and, as a further mark of respect, his gun-belt too.

The girl rang downstairs for some coffee and cookies. These arrived in charge of a diminutive Chinese boy and, when he had left, the three old friends settled down to a real chinwag.

Yes, Ron Purcell remembered Maria now. But not this Maria! Now he was discovering her all over again and the discovery was sweet.

She talked intelligently, kept pace with the two men. She did not blanch when, in answer to a forthright question from Jeff, Ron told how he had gotten the scar on his face. He painted tersely but vividly a picture of that night in Dodge City when he and three other men had tried to prevent a lynching and had almost gotten lynched themselves in the process. The mutilating scar had come from the very knife with which Ron Purcell had slashed the hempen rope in two: it had been snatched from him and turned against him by a member of the mob.

'What happened to him?' asked the girl.

'I got the knife back,' replied the man simply.

Her face was grave but she met his gaze boldly. Maybe, though he might not even have admitted it to himself, he was testing her. A real frontierswoman did not blench at such tales of violence. This one, it seemed, had already won her spurs. You could not expect anything else of the daughter of the staunch Jeff Laing. He had been a lawman and Government scout before he took up ranchiag. His wife had been killed by Indians when Maria was only a baby. He was older than he looked, was Jeff; he carried his age well, strutting like a bantam-cock.

It was Jeff's early training that had helped to launch the boy, Ron, on his hazardous calling as a troubleshooter – sometimes officially; sometimes otherwise. (Now he was getting older Ron wasn't so proud of the latter assignments, they smacked too much of professional gunmanship). He sometimes wondered whether he was really any better than a hired killer like Kid Stone, after all. Even the Kid, as deadly and pitiless as a rattlesnake though he was, always gave a man an even break.

Young Ron Purcell, an orphan after losing both parents in a stage-coach accident, applied at Jeff Laing's spread for a job and got it. Even at sixteen he was a good ranch-hand, even as his father, an inveterate globe-trotter, had been before him. Old Jeff had never had a son; he took to the boy, taught him how to take care of himself as only an old Western lawman (their watchword eternal vigilance) could.

It was inevitable that Ron, a spirited youth, should finally seek fresh fields for adventure. But Jeff, as evidenced by the warm welcome he gave his erstwhile protégé now, had not held this against him.

'You've certainly gotten around since we met last, son,' the old rancher said.

Not long afterwards he rose. 'I've got to go down the street to meet a man,' he said. 'It's just business – it'd bore you, Maria – but if you an' Ron would like to shake your legs with me so far, Ron could walk you back here afterwards.'

This was agreed upon. Trappings were donned once more and they set out. The girl had changed her riding-togs for a dress which, despite its fashionable frills and furbelows, fitted her trim, healthy figure like a glove. A bright, plaid blanket-coat finished her ensemble. Saying it was a beautiful night, she went hatless.

Although Ron was a little scared that Mike might send to the hotel for him while he was out, he couldn't very well refuse the walk. It would've been discourteous to a lady. Besides, he liked walking with her. Anyway, Ron figured that, judging by the headway Duke had been making, he was stuck with that poker-school for the rest of the evening. Duke was too good a sportsman, and too avid a gambler, to quit halfway through the night while he was winning.

Ron and the girl left Jeff at the little rooming house at the end of the main drag where the rancher had to meet his business acquaintance. Then, not talking much, they walked slowly back to the hotel.

As they approached the doors a man came lurching out.

'Oh,' said Maria involuntarily, then with an undercurrent of amusement in her voice, 'Here's that awful young man called Dobbs.'

It was the younger of the three cattle-buyers, the

big sullen-looking one. So this was Dobbs was it? Where were Messrs. Spingle and Crane, then – and which was which?

The burly young man lurched against Ron, almost knocking him against the girl. Ron didn't know whether it was deliberate or not, but it could've been.

No apology came, so Ron turned on the man. 'Watch where you're going.'

'Don't block the way, then,' was the snarling reply.

Here was a *hombre* who for some obscure reason carried a mansized chip. Here was a real mean one. His fists balled, Ron turned again.

Maria grabbed his arm, pulled at it. 'Don't brawl with him, Ron,' she urged. 'He's drunk.'

There were other people around: Ron didn't want to create a scene in which Maria would probably be embroiled, so he held his peace. Then, as they were passing through the door, the thick jeering voice called, 'Take care o' the li'l lady, won't you, pardner.'

Ron made to turn again but, with surprising strength, Maria pushed him forward and the door closed behind them.

The young man almost lost his temper with her. As they went up the stairs he asked a harsh and abrupt question: 'Has that galoot been pestering you?'

'He goes out of his way to be polite if that's what you mean,' she replied tartly. 'And he *does* go out of his way.'

'If that's a sample of his politeness I don't cotton

to it,' said Ron. He decided he would look up Mr Dobbs.

He disregarded the girl's anxious look and said `Good night' to her at the door. There were some things a woman just couldn't stop a man from doing. Maria, a frontierswoman born and bred, could not help but know this. She did not call after him as he went down the stairs.

Outside, Dobbs had vanished from sight. Ron decided he'd check on Duke first of all anyway. Mr Dobbs would keep.

CHAPTER IX

When he entered Tombstone Mike's place he was surprised to see Dobbs leaning against the bar. He had assumed automatically that the burly young cattle-buyer had been making for The Golden Lizard.

Dobbs had his two pardners with him, Spingle and Crane. Ron remembered now that Mike had told him these three used his place quite often.

Dobbs was leering at the young ranny. It was almost as if he had been waiting for him, waiting for an opponent. He had the bearing of a seasoned brawler. Maybe he just had to prove his prowess in every town he hit.

Ron glanced over towards the poker table. The game was still in session. Duke looked up, caught his eye, winked. The little dude still seemed to be winning.

Ron moved on to the bar, inclined his head politely to the three men, finally fixed his gaze wholly on the younger one.

'Mr Dobbs?'

'That's me.'

'I'd like a few words with you in private – outside.'

Dobbs leered again. 'If you've got anything to say to me, mister, you can say it right here.' His fingers were curled around his glass, half-full of liquor, on the bar beside him. Ron noticed this fact as he moved in a little closer. He said:

'I don't like men who insult ladies. I don't like men who insult me when I'm with a lady. I don't like you, Mr Dobbs. I think you're a blundering ox with the heart of a coyote. You stink, Mr Dobbs.'

The big man moved, the glass with it. Ron swayed to one side, felt a few spots of liquor burn into his cheek, soak through his shirt at the shoulder. The raw tang of it smote his nostrils like a blow, uncoiling the savagery within him. Swaying forward a little now he rammed both fists into Dobbs' stomach, one after the other. Dobbs grunted and bent forward and Ron backed swiftly, realizing the sullen man's two pards were moving in on him from both sides. He ducked under a blow that Spingle (or was it Crane?) flung at him. Then a voice rang out:

'Break it up – or I'll start shooting.'

Ron backed a little more, in order to get things in a proper perspective, then froze in his tracks. The other two men, their heads half-turned, were frozen too. And between them, half-crouched, his hands held before him, Dobbs was immobile, his eyes gazing at Ron Purcell in pain and hate.

Tombstone Mike was leaning over the bar, a sawn-off shotgun cradled in his hands.

'If there's gonna be fighting it's gotta be outside,'

he said. 'I'm not gonna have my place wrecked.'

'All right, Mike,' said Ron Purcell, and, turning his back deliberately on the three men, began to walk towards the door.

Duke Linstone had left the card-table and ranged himself beside Ron. Then without a word, he dropped a little behind his pardner. Ron realized the reason for this manoeuvre when, on reaching the boardwalk, he turned. Duke had a gun at the back of Spingle and Crane and was relieving them of their weapons.

'This is gonna be a straight fight between my friend and the big boy,' he said. 'Anybody who tries to horn in will get his hide perforated.'

The dude cowboy probably didn't know what it was all about but he meant to back his pardner regardless. Ron Purcell reflected sardonically that this would at least serve to keep Duke out of mischief in other directions.

'Thanks, pardner,' he said, and handed his own gunbelt over.

Dobbs had gotten over the buffeting in the belly that he had received.

'I can handle this puppy,' he said in a loud voice.

Then he, too, handed over his armoury. The whole caboodle was given to a bright-eyed youth to hold. Duke stood with one hand on his own reholstered gun and his eyes on Spingle and Crane. The news had spread. Already folks were approaching from all directions, as well as streaming out of Tombstone Mike's place. Mike himself could be seen at his window. But he still cradled his shotgun in case he needed it.

Dobbs took off his slouch hat and handed it to one of his *compadres*. He stripped off his leather vest and his shirt with the slow, smouldering deliberation of the seasoned brawler. There was an air of malignant anticipation about him.

Ron Purcell had retreated to the centre of main street. Now he too divested himself of his hat (the new one he had only bought that morning), his vest and his shirt. He handed these to the youth who had been waiting tentatively to receive them.

This worthy grinned. 'Give him heck, Mr Purcell.'

Ron nodded. One side of his mouth curled up in a cold grin, twisting the scar, until his face, with the narrowed killer's eyes, had a wolfish appearance.

The crowd was becoming thicker now as the news went round town that there was gonna be a fight by Tombstone Mike's place. This kind of premeditated mill was something almost alien to Rampage: fights here usually took the form of hurried brawls in barrooms, many of which ended in shooting, in killing. This one might end in killing too, but, at least, it was bound to be far bloodier than usual.

Purcell, the Loop V boy, had the reputation of being a real mean one with a gun. Now was his chance to prove whether he was just as handy with his maulies.

The Rampage folks didn't know the other boy but he looked a real mean one too. And, with his barrel-like chest festooned with black hairs, his sullen, lumpy, lopsided face, he looked like a man who, despite his comparative youth, had done his share of milling.

The crowd formed a rough circle, tightpacked, a thick ring of faces, of jostling bodies, of yammering shouting mouths. They packed the sidewalks each side of the main drag, packed the street in a solid mass except for the space in the centre.

'Give 'em room!' yelled somebody. 'Give 'em room!'

The crowd fluctuated, tightened. Men cursed. Somewhere a woman screamed. Lights streamed from the windows of Tombstone Mike's place and from another establishment on the other side of the street. For added illumination somebody had hung a couple of hurricane lanterns high on fence-posts. A buggy, drawn by two horses, came along the street. Perched on its high seat were a weather-beaten elderly couple. Their way was blocked. They looped the reins up and sat there, the old man leaning forward avidly, his gums champing rhythmically on his chew. Him and the missus had a good view up there anyway.

The yellow stream from the windows, the fluctuating glow of the lanterns, bathed the scene in a dancing, garish light. The two contestants moved slowly towards each other in the time-honoured way, their boots going *scuff-scuff* in the dust, in the sudden silence. They circled warily, still almost too far apart to do any harm.

Dobbs used the stance adopted by most famous bare-knuckle fighters of the day. His hands were up, his fists clenched, the knuckles pointing towards his opponent. His arms were bent stiffly at the elbows. His knees were bent too, the right one out in front of the other, so that he was spraddled a little. Although his torso was stiffly upright, the bent knees lowered his height considerably. The whole stance, pugnaciously fashionable though it was, the stance of the professional or semi-professional, had a doll-like stiffness about it. Also, Dobbs's elbows were so high up that they served no protection for his stomach. Maybe, considering the way his opponent had already punished that rather sizeable target, Dobbs should have had more sense.

Purcell didn't adopt anything that might have been called a stance. He moved forward in a catlike sort of way, with his hands waving in front of him, his fists only loosely balled. As they circled each other, he moved in a more supple way, on the balls of his feet, but with no evidence in his bearing that he had ever had any pugilistic training.

His opponent, however, most evidently had: and now began to put it into practice. He moved on his man suddenly, his feet going *slap-slap* in the dust. He snaked out a right fist, buffeting Purcell's shoulder, making him stagger. Purcell had moved fast too, and there had been a miscalculation. But now Dobbs follow-up left landed with a smack on the side of Purcell's jaw and there was a savage collective 'Oh' from the crowd.

Purcell was teetering and Dobbs bored after him. But Purcell weaved away and then came in from the side, hooking a right into Dobbs's middle, a left to the side of his head. Then dancing round in front of him, seeming to throw blows from all angles.

The crowd made a noise like the baying of wolves. Then, as Dobbs recovered himself and the two men stood almost toe-to-toe, swapping blows, the noise began to break up into ragged, savage fragments as men urged their favourites on.

Shriller womens' voices sometimes rang above the din, for most of the girls of the town, good-naturedly running the gauntlet of pinches and squeezes, had worked their way to the front.

Ron Purcell staggered backwards. 'Don't let him crowd yuh, pard,' yelled Duke Linstone urgently.

Dobbs charged bull-like after his opponent, but once more, shaking blood from his face, Purcell eluded him, was waiting for him when he turned. They came together again and the blows were sickeningly hard, flat; at times sounding almost like pistol shots.

The crowd had quietened a little now and only gave vent from time to time to a collective gasp; or a roar of approval when a particularly cunning blow was struck.

The two contestants moved apart again, weaving a little, catching their breath. They were beginning to show the marks of the battle.

Blood had dried on Purcell's face. The scar there, too, seemed to writhe like a living thing in the flickering light, giving him an almost demoniacal appearance. His body, leaner and less hairy than his opponent's, but wideshouldered and deep-chested, bore red marks on its tan. Blood from his face had dappled it too. With this warpaint, and locks of his long hair falling over his forehead, he looked almost like a savage Indian brave.

Dobbs's body revealed less damage because of the

matted black hair that decorated it. He had a cut under his eye however, and his nose had been bleeding. His eyes gleamed with hate. He looked like a savage fighting ape.

Sheriff Brighouse suddenly appeared on the outskirts of the crowd, behind him Kid Stone.

As usual the portly lawman did not seem quite sober. 'What's going on?' he demanded querulously. 'Let me through! Stop it!'

'Keep out o' this, sheriff,' yelled somebody. 'It's a fair fight.'

'That's the best way to settle anything ain't it?' shouted somebody else. 'An' by the way they're goin' on it don't look like there'll be any jail-meat left for you.'

A roar of laughter greeted this sally. The sheriff was pushed and prodded playfully. At any other time the presence of his yellow-haired friend with the vulture's eyes, the notorious Kid Stone, might have saved him from such treatment, but the crowd were in force and enjoying themselves too much to take any notice of a single killer. Mayhem on a grand scale was going on again in the middle of the circle. They forgot the sheriff, allowing him to worm his way, with the help of his companion, into a spot from whence they could both see the fight.

Kid Stone enjoined his companion to stay put, not to stick his chin out. This looked like being good. It was good!

The two contestants were milling once more with a savage brutality. Dobbs' arms worked liked pistons with a hammer at the end of each one. He wasn't bothering where he hit his opponent now – just so long as he hit him. Realizing that, despite his lack of any proper stance, this lean ranny was no mean opponent, he was trying to batter him into submission with sheer brute force.

The other man looked a pretty gory mess. But he wouldn't keep still: he still capered around like an Indian brave.

Dobbs had relinquished his fancy stonewalling tactics. Any similarity to a stance which could be noticed about him now was purely accidental. He tried to smother his opponent and guard himself at the same time with a barrage of blows. But Purcell kept getting beneath that guard and hammering at the big man's middle, which was beginning to look like a slab of raw meat.

Dobbs's feet went *slap-slap* in the dust. His knees were no longer bent. He stiffened them like ramrods in an effort to prevent himself from lurching forward. He contracted his stomach to try and counteract the sickness and agony that was beating at him in waves.

He didn't lack guts, however, and kept boring in. He had the satisfaction of realizing that his opponent was weakening too, was teetering, bending at the knees. He lashed out with a haymaker and felt a cruel satisfaction as it connected.

Ron Purcell was sent sprawling in the dust. The lights spun around him, the roaring of the crowd was like a stampede of cattle bearing down on him as he lay helpless. The white yammering faces, spinning around him like a myriad flabby white balloons, seemed to mock him.

Only a sixth sense saved him from having his face caved in by Dobbs' heavy swinging boot. He rolled, a gust of rage seizing him, bringing new strength. The cries of the crowd had changed. Many people did not like Dobbs' cowardly move, the fight had been fair up till this.

Now a roar of approval went up as Purcell grabbed hold of Dobbs' ankle with both hands and pulled. Dobbs did a neat parabola and came down with a crash that raised a mansized cloud of dust and seemed to make the very ground vibrate.

Purcell rose to his feet, levering himself upwards with both hands pressed against the ground. He shook his head like a wounded animal, his long brown hair flopping over his eyes. A few drops of blood spattered in the dust. Slowly he straightened up to his full height, stood teetering a little, his hands hanging at his sides as he looked down at his fallen opponent.

Puffing and blowing like a grampus – a creature that none of the watchers, denizens of the great plains, had ever seen – Dobbs was slowly beginning to rise again. He rose to one knee, then higher . . .

'Finish him, Purcell!' shouted an almost hysterical voice. 'Finish him!'

But Ron Purcell continued to stand there, drawing air into his chest in great gulps, building up his strength, waiting. He seemed to renew his suppleness, and a latent savagery, as he waited. Waited like a beast, tensing his muscles for a spring; and the final annihilating blow.

But Dobbs it seemed was not beaten yet. He had the strength of a bull and, now that his fury had dimmed, the cunning of a fox too. He rose to full stature with rapidity, and charged. Purcell met him with both fists flying but did not have a chance to deliver that well-placed blow.

The two men closed, wrestled. Dobbs threw Purcell from him with brute force but was a little too fast in charging after him, hands clawing to rend and tear. Purcell, although he was almost on his knees, managed to scramble away. Dobbs shot past him, head first into the crowd. Right into the spot where his two pardners stood.

When he turned, rushed at Ron Purcell again, he had a knife uplifted in his hand. Ron saw the hate-filled eyes. They seemed to gleam redly with murder. He tried to dodge the gleaming arc of the down-sweeping blade. His foot twisted in the churning dust.

He felt the steel bite into his shoulder, first cold, then agonizingly hot. He flung his hand up desperately, aiming for Dobbs' wrist but almost screaming when his fingers closed over the naked blade. He felt himself falling, the lights spinning around him again, the screaming faces.

He tried to save himself from falling, his bleeding fingers digging into the ground. He did not know that Dobbs hit the ground, flatly, even before he did.

Duke Linstone, enraged and scandalised by the big fella's treachery, had beaten him over the head with a gun-butt.

CHAPTER X

Half-dazed, Ron was carried into Tombstone Mike's place and up into one of the bedrooms.

Doc Logan was sent for and came post-haste. He awakened Ron completely by swabbing his wounds with some cold stinging liquid.

The young cowhand's mutilated hand and his punctured shoulder were swathed in bandages and his arm was put in a sling. He was allowed to sit up and smoke but was told to stay in bed for a while. His gunhand was slashed – doc said it was lucky none of the 'guides' were cut but he couldn't say for sure yet whether it would mend properly or not. It was his right shoulder that was damaged too. Doc Logan said the wound, though deep, was straight and clean and he hoped that it would heal that way.

The hand was the worst job though! After the doc had gone Ron sat up in bed, dragging at a cigarette and looking at the misshapen lump of white bandage. He was like an eagle with a broken wing. He felt totally helpless. He had never realized till now how much he really depended on that good right hand of his.

Now more than ever it seemed he needed that good right hand, the gun it could hold, the fist it could form. He felt a bitter frustration; and a rage so great against the treacherous Dobbs that he felt like leaping out of bed and going to find the man, to beat him to a pulp with the other hand that was left; and his feet too, if need be.

Still, by all accounts Dobbs was laid up, too; that was some consolation. Tombstone Mike had told Ron of how Duke Linstone had beaten the big fellow over the head with a gun-butt, thus probably saving Ron's life: Dobbs had acted like a maniac before he had been finally poleaxed. Dobbs's two pardners had carted him back to his lodgings.

Ron wondered if Maria Laing had heard about the shindig by now and what were her feelings about it. He had looked around for Duke, in order to thank him. Duke was nowhere around. Mike said the little dude wasn't downstairs either. Somebody said that as soon as Duke had made sure his pardner wasn't going to cash in his chips he had left the place.

Ron was worried about the volatile little cowhand. To try and set his mind at rest, Mike promised to send a man out looking for Duke, to bring him back if possible. Ron tried to get out of bed, but the effort almost made him pass out again. Dobbs had certainly been a handful. Apart from his wounds, Ron had aches and bruises which made him feel like he had tangled with a grizzly bear. He could only sit there, propped up on a mound of pillows like a doggoned invalid, and hope for the best.

Mike reappeared after a while with some hot coffee, a can of biscuits and half a bottle of whiskey. Ron took a glass of the latter to begin with. The raw hooch stung his puffed lips. He hadn't taken a look at himself in a mirror but, judging by the quantity of lint and tape with which Doc Logan had embell-ished him, he figured he was quite a sight.

'Any news of Duke yet, Mike?' he asked.

'Nope. Don't worry – Duke can take care of himself.'

'Yeh, I guess so.'

'I best go back to my bar I guess,' said Mike. 'Is there anything else you want, kid? Will you be all right?'

'Roll me a couple of smokes before you go will you? I ain't partial to these store things.' Ron grinned ruefully. 'And I'm afraid I'm not in any condition now to roll my own.'

'Sure thing. Sure.'

Mike took the makings and set to work. He rolled Ron half-a-dozen neat fat quirlies and lit one up for him before taking his leave once more.

Ron puffed away as the door closed. His gratitude to Mike was replaced by rage at the man and the circumstances that had brought him to this pass. Couldn't even make his own smokes now. A fine troubleshooter he'd turned out to be. He had once reformed, gone back to nursing dogies. It was a pity he hadn't stayed that way, it was all he was good for! He felt like a lame duck.

He smoked furiously. His body ached for sleep but his restless mind would not allow this. He had refused the sedative Doc Logan offered him.

'If you spend too much time wrestling with yourself your temperature will soar again an' you'll run a fever,' the doc had told him.

Probably, the doc was right. Ron stubbed out his fourth cigarette and slid lower beneath the bedclothes. It was getting late. The sounds from outside were diminishing. Every now and then horsemen clattered by, homeward-bound.

Ron straightened up hurriedly when he heard footsteps on the stairs.

The door opened and Tombstone Mike came in.

The old lawdog was grinning all over his craggy face. 'A lady to see you, Mistuh Purcell,' he announced. He made a flourish. 'Miss Maria Laing.'

Maria came into view. Mike withdrew, closing the door gently behind him.

Maria came closer to the bed. She looked anxious; but Ron didn't figure she was mad at him. He took a chance and grinned, though the effort made him feel as if his face was breaking in half.

'Will you take a seat, ma'am,' he said gravely.

She smiled, dimpling. She sat down on the bedside chair. 'How are you feeling, Ron?'

'Could be worse I guess.'

'You shouldn't have tangled with that ape. You might've known he wouldn't play fair.'

Ron made a gesture with his good hand. 'What else could I do?'

Maria had been brought up in the West, she knew

its unwritten code. She knew there was only one answer to that question, so she made no further comment.

'Dad will be up to see you soon. He left me. I think he's buying you a bunch of flowers or something.'

Ron grinned. 'I'll bet.' This was the kind of girl he liked. No slop. Treating a man the way he liked to be treated after he had been in the fight, the way a man-friend would treat him, the best way.

Beneath the bantering pose she was all feminine though a man would have to be blind to miss that. And there was something in her dark eyes that made Ron's stomach turn over.

She said softly, but with that same bantering tone, 'It all comes back to me now, Sir Galahad. When I was a kid you were my hero, my knight-errant. I never thought then that one day you'd go out jousting on my account.'

Ron got a little flustered. 'That ape insulted us both,' he said.

The girl pouted. 'Oh, don't spoil it.'

He grinned, resuming his equilibrium. He reached out with his good hand and gripped hers. 'I never thought that lanky imp in pigtails would turn out to be such a lovely lady. With such a honeyed tongue, too.'

'I went to college back East for a couple of years you know. One of the things they taught me was dramatic art. I even took parts in a couple of school plays.'

'Did you like it back there?'

'Not much.' She laughed. 'Too many milksops,

male and female; I'm afraid I was too much of a country cousin. I was glad to get back home.' Her eyes glowed. 'I love this country. There's something missing when I'm away from it. I hate these Eastern cities and their fancy ways, their new-fangled motor-cars, their habit of never saying what they really think . . .'

'I bet you knocked 'em for a loop,' said Ron admiringly.

What might have transpired after this is hard to predict, but now more footsteps sounded on the stairs and Ron let go of Maria's hand.

Jeff Laing came in. He had paused, not to get flowers, but a box of the finest cheroots in town.

'Son!' he chortled. 'You certainly showed that cowardly snake a thing or two. He ain't come to his senses yet.'

'That's mostly due to my pard, Duke, I'm afraid,' said Ron. 'He ain't very big but he's got the strength of a mule.'

As Duke Linstone helped to carry his insensible pard into Tombstone Mike's place, he spotted Kid Stone among the crowd and there was brought back to him the reason why he had come into Rampage to-night in the first place. Now he became mad because he had let himself be sidetracked by a game of poker. He had come into town to get to the bottom of the killing of Pete Manetti.

Ron Purcell had been told Pete was killed in self-defence, beaten to the draw by Kid Stone. That might well be! Pete had been fast, but the Kid was one of the fastest. The pale-faced yellow-haired gambler made his living by sleight-of-hand in more ways than one. The Kid also had the reputation of always giving the other man an even break; most times he could well afford to. But Ron Purcell had admitted that he hadn't been in Lemmy's Place when the shooting had happened. He had only gone by hearsay.

Duke did not doubt Ron. Far from it. But he was a ornery little cuss, he wanted to find out things for himself, judge things for himself. He had wondered if the sheriff was going to do anything about the killing. But evidently not: the two of them had been hobnobbing together as usual, Duke had spotted the sheriff at Kid Stone's elbow there among the crowd. The fact of a lawman tagging along like a jackal with a notorious killer was pretty suspicious. Maybe there had been some kind of frame-up, with Pete Manetti as the sucker. The way, maybe, that Walt Crisp had been a sucker, and Hank Butler.

Duke meant to do some investigating. If the law was useless, a man had to be law himself sometimes. Duke was quite prepared to call out Kid Stone. Right then the fact that the notorious gunfighter might haze him never entered his head, or, if it did, was neatly sidestepped. Pete Manetti had been reckoned as Duke's friend. If the truth were told Duke liked Ron Purcell better. There had been something cold and brutal about the taciturn Peter, and he had wanted to take on Kid Stone from the time he first saw him. But Pete had been Duke's saddle-partner for a long time. A man just didn't let down his saddle-partner, alive or dead. There were some things a man just had to do regardless of consequences.

Duke waited until Doc Logan had pronounced the patient to be still alive, and liable to be kicking any minute, then went out on his quest.

Little knots of men were still gathered in the street before Tombstone Mike's place. A fight such as they had just watched had not happened to them many times before. They relived it now as they would relive it again in time to come, champing on their baccy-stained whiskers as they told the story to their grandchildren.

There was no sign of Spingle and Crane and their unconscious pardner. Nor of Sheriff Sam Brighouse and Kid Stone.

Duke moved unobtrusively along the boardwalk, going in the opposite direction to Lemmy Macklein's Golden Lizard Saloon.

He reached the edge of town. The lights did not reach him now. There was nobody around. He crossed the street, moved behind the backs of Main Street. He reached the back of Lemmy's Place. It was in darkness, though from the front came the sound of excited voices, men and girls returning from the fight. Duke tried a door. It opened at his touch and he passed through it and into darkness.

He stood for a moment until his eyes became accustomed to this new consistency of blackness. Finally he learned he was in one of the kitchens. One that wasn't used much either by the look of it. It smelled, too, of stale food, stale air. Moving catlike, Duke found another door and opened it.

He was in a passage. There was another door to the right of him and a third at the end of the passage. Beneath this one was a thread of yellow light. Duke stood still for a moment, listening, his hand on the butt of his gun.

He hadn't spotted Lemmy at the fight. The snaky saloon-keeper certainly hadn't been with Kid Stone and the sheriff. Duke figured that if he caught the saloon-keeper alone maybe he'd find out the truth about the gunplay this morning. He hadn't a settled plan in his mind, but if he had an excuse to push Lemmy's face in again he would be highly delighted. Lemmy might be the Grand Panjandrum here in town but he didn't awe a Loop V boy. Duke had given ample evidence of that last night and was quite willing to labour the point. He catfooted along the passage and pressed his ear to the door of the lighted room.

Although the sounds from the front of the saloon were louder now, there didn't seem to be anything moving inside the room. However, Duke drew his gun before finally sliding the door open.

He found himself in an office. The yellow light burned down on the wide, empty mahogany desk, the ornate bookshelves, on the turkey-red carpet into which Duke's feet sank as he moved forward.

This was Lemmy's office all right: Lemmy liked luxury. Probably he had been working in here when he heard the disturbance and he had gone out to investigate, leaving the door unlocked, the light burning behind him. It was very careless of him!

Duke closed the door softly behind him. Gun in hand, he made a circuit of the room. The heavy red velvet curtains were drawn at the window. Probably not a chink of light was revealed outside.

Duke glanced at the titles of the books in the shelves. Some of them were familiar to him; others puzzled him a little. Shakespeare's plays; the poems of Byron, of Tennyson, of Longfellow; The Life of Nelson; The Origin of Species; The Anatomy of Melancholy; the Man; and others, many others. They stood behind glass, fatly, richly bound in glossy varicoloured leather with gold lettering that hurt the eyes to look at it. They looked as if they had never been opened. In fact, the ornate bookcases looked as if they had never been opened either, as if the whole caboodle had been carted here this way and set down, to dazzle the simple Westerners with its magnificence.

Duke spat drily. He paused before a tall thing of glossy wood. It seemed to be nothing more than a pile of little drawers. Although Duke did not know it, this was the newest Eastern idea in filing-cabinets.

Duke tried all the little drawers one by one. They were all locked. He tried to prise them open with his gunbarrel, then with his clasp-knife. They were fitted stoutly and resisted all his endeavours. Disgusted, he turned last of all to the desk.

He tried the huge middle drawer. This was locked too. He tried the others, two rows, four on each side. They were all locked except the top one on the left-hand side. This was full of papers and oddments.

Placing his gun on the desk in front of him, Duke began his investigations.

The stuff was mostly bills to do with Lemmy's ownership and managing of The Golden Lizard. They told Duke very little that he didn't already know, or had guessed. Then in the bottom, to where the smaller stuff had gradually sifted, he found stubs from a cheque book. He flipped through them. Most of the stubs bore names which he had already come across in the bills. Until he came to the very last one.

This bore the name Leslie E. Stone. The familiar 'Stone' rang a bell in Duke's mind right away, but it was some seconds before he remembered that Kid Stone's name was Leslie, the sheriff had called him 'Les' the other night.

Duke knew that the Kid was working for Lemmy; the sick-looking killer had himself made no secret of that fact. But this stub was dated almost a month ago, long before the Kid had arrived in Rampage. And why should Lemmy Macklein be paying the professional gambler and gunfighter the princely sum of three thousand dollars so soon?

Duke put the stubs into his pocket and began to run the rest of the stuff through his fingers to make sure he hadn't missed anything. A torn fragment of paper fluttered to the floor. Duke bent and picked it up. It was a piece of lined notepaper and a portion of a sentence was inscribed upon it in a spidery handwriting.

'. . . *his real name is Garnett, and was then.*'

Nothing more. And though Duke rummaged

through the drawer he could not find another piece to this jigsaw. Probably it was part of a letter that Lemmy had written and then torn up, a piece of it inadvertently falling into the open drawer. The handwriting was unmistakably the same as that in the writing on the bank stubs. Had Lemmy ever sent a letter with that name 'Garnett' in it? A name that set Duke Linstone's brain racing a mile a minute!

He folded the fragment of notepaper and inserted it carefully into his vest pocket. He tidied the drawer until he hoped it looked like the the way he had found it. He closed the drawer, picked up his gun, with a last look around the room, crossed to the door. He leaned against it, listening. Out front the revellers were having their last fling and already 'good-nights' were being shouted. A few seconds later Duke Linstone was in the darkness out back. He hadn't seen a soul.

He began to walk among the ashcans and the scrub grass. He was almost at the end of town when he sensed the presence of somebody else near him. He reached for his gun, beginning to turn at the same time.

Something slammed him hard below the left shoulder blade. A ball of flame blossomed there and burst. He felt no more. He did not even hear the shot.

Nobody else had heard the shot either. It was much later that a late drinker, stumbling along in the silence, tripped over his body and raised the alarm.

When they broke the news to Ron Purcell he had to be forcibly restrained from leaving his bed and shooting the town up – left-handed.

CHAPTER XI

The following morning Sheriff Brighouse paid Ron a visit. Kid Stone trailed along too, like a pale, rather malevolent shadow.

The wounded cowboy greeted them curtly. He looked Kid Stone over with eyes that were hard and watchful. 'We're might sorry about Duke,' said the sheriff, his walrus moustache drooping mournfully.

Ron Purcell said nothing.

Kid Stone did not say anything either.

A little uncertainly, the sheriff went on, standing in front of the bed as if in supplication, his belly spilling over his trouser-top. 'We thought you'd like to know what we've found out.'

'Have yuh found out anything?' said Ron Purcell flatly.

The sheriff shuffled his feet, finally sat down on the chair beside the bed. Kid Stone remained standing, his thumbs hooked in his belt. He didn't seem to be looking at anything in particular. The sheriff was sober and, lacking Dutch courage, rather ill at ease.

He cleared his throat, the noise falling explosively in the waiting stillness. Then he said:

'We haven't found any clue as to who killed him, but we do know he was robbed. His body was picked clean, except for his gun. The filthy skunk took no chances. Duke never had a chance to turn round or get his gun out.'

He paused as if waiting for Ron or the Kid to speak. Neither of them did, so, after a moment's hesitation, he went on again: 'I'm told that Duke won a sizeable pot in a poker game here last night. That is so, ain't it, Ron?'

This time the cowboy had to answer him. 'I wasn't in the game, but, yeh, he looked like he was winning to me.'

'I spoke to two of the men who were playing with him,' said the sheriff. 'He'd taken them for quite a bit. There wasn't a cent on him.'

'You think robbery was the motive for the killing, then?'

'It suttinly looks like it. Though I guess the body could've been robbed in order to put us off the track.'

'That's a good deduction, sheriff,' said Ron Purcell sardonically. 'Have you investigated the other possibilities then: that Duke was shot by somebody who hated him, or wanted to shut his mouth?'

'I'm doing my best, son,' said Sam Brighouse, and for a moment there was a new-found dignity about him. 'I want to get the skunk who bushwhacked Duke just as much as you do.'

'Yeh, I guess you do,' said the man in bed.

His voice did not carry any conviction, however; it was dull, almost lifeless. Maybe that remark about 'getting' Duke's killer had brought home to him his own inability at the moment to tackle this task himself.

Sam Brighouse said: 'What I can't figure is what Duke was doing round the back of town in that particular spot.'

Ron Purcell had a pretty good idea what Duke had been doing round there. But he did not voice his idea. And the sheriff went on:

'Maybe he saw somebody acting suspiciously and tailed them an' they fooled him somehow an' got in behind. Maybe somebody got him out there purposely in order to bushwhack him.'

'That hardly seems feasible,' said Kid Stone, speaking for the first time. 'By what I've seen of Duke he was a pretty cunning little galoot.'

Ron Purcell's hard eyes were turned on the pale-faced gun-fighter again, remained fixed there. The Kid returned their gaze levelly. 'Let me ask you a question, Ron,' he said.

'Go ahead.'

'Did Duke go out gunning for me last night because I killed his friend, Pete?'

'Could be.'

'So!' said Kid softly. He paused for a moment as both men watched him; then he went on again: 'You've known me a long time, Ron. We've met up in a strange variety of places. Have you ever known me to shoot a man in the back?'

Ron Purcell found himself replying instantly, 'No!'

The sheriff broke in. 'Les! He hasn't accused you of . . .'

'Let me handle this, Sam.' The Kid bent his gaze on Ron once more. 'As Duke helped you into this place last night after the fight,' he smiled thinly, '– you certainly showed that big ape a thing or two, pardner – he turned and positively glared at me. Maybe after he had seen you were well taken care of he came out looking for me.'

'Could be,' said Ron again. 'But that ain't to say that he was gunning for yuh. Maybe he didn't believe in hearsay, maybe he wanted to get the truth of his pard's death from the man who caused it.'

'He probably wouldn't have found me anyway,' said Kid Stone. 'After the fight I went right back to Sam's office with him.'

'Huh,' said Ron. 'What's the matter with you lately, Kid, you sold out to the law or somep'n? You claim to be a dealer or somep'n for Lemmy Macklein but you seem to spend most of your time playing wet-nurse to the sheriff.'

'I resent . . .' began Sam Brighouse. But once more the Kid cut him short.

'He's a nosey son of a sea-calf is Ron, but I guess we better tell him the truth, Sam. It won't do any harm.'

'It might complicate things if other people know, though,' protested Sam.

'I think we can trust Ron to keep his mouth shut.'

'Les is my nephew,' said Sam hoarsely. 'My sister's boy. He just came to look me up. He says I need a sort of unofficial deputy in this stinking town.' His voice became plaintive. 'I been kinda sick lately, Ron. An old wound in my side is playing me up. The pain drives me half-crazy sometimes.'

'Have yuh seen Doc Logan?'

'I didn't want anybody to know. I didn't want folks to think I was cracking up.'

Ron's private opinion was that people already thought that; laughed at the sheriff for a drink-sodden old has-been. Still, maybe Sam drank to kill the pain, maybe there was some excuse for the old buzzard.

'Does all that answer one of your questions, Ron?' asked Kid Stone.

'I guess so,' said the man in the bed. 'Let's get back to Duke Linstone, then. Have you found any clues?'

'Not a thing.' The sheriff paused, clearing his throat nervously. Then he said: 'We saw Duke slug that Dobbs crittur when he knifed you. We checked on Dobbs and his two pards. Dobbs was in no condition to go around shooting people in the back and his two pards were with him all evening. Leastways, the desk-clerk didn't see either of 'em go out. Had Duke any other enemies, Ron?'

'Any man's liable to have enemies. Though Duke was a pretty friendly, likeable sort of cuss unless he was roused.' Ron added slowly, 'He had a fight in Lemmy's Place the other night, though, didn't he?'

The sheriff cleared his throat again but no words followed. It was Kid Stone who said softly, 'Lemmy and Mose. Yeh, I guess we better check on them, huh?'

Ron Purcell heard himself saying, 'I thought Lemmy was your friend.'

'Not if he goes around shooting people in the back!'

Little more was said after this and presently the two men left.

Ron was still wondering on the enigma of Kid Stone, gunfighter par excellence, when his next visitors arrived.

One of them was Mike, bearing a steaming hot meal and a jug of coffee. Also two cups: one for Ron, the other for Burt Cooley, ramrod of the Loop V.

'I wish you wouldn't wait on me yourself like this, Mike,' said Ron.

'You deserve it, son,' grinned Mike. 'I'm paying now for that ringside seat I had at the best fight I've ever seen in my life. When you're better I'll go out an' see if I can break my leg. Then, I promise you, I'll let you wait on line.'

'I'll hold you to that,' said Ron, and, as Mike left the room, turned to the foreman.

'Sit down, Burt. Make yourself at home.'

Burt Cooley seated himself a little uncomfortably on the bedside chair. 'How yuh feelin', Ron?' he asked.

'Could be worse I guess.'

'The old man asked me tuh come along an' see yuh . . .' Burt's voice tailed off.

Ron eyed him quizzically. 'Did he now? That was very thoughtful of him.'

'You won't say that when you hear what else I have to tell yuh,' said Burt, adding hastily, 'Still, I aimed to come along an' see you myself anyway. I guess most of the boys'll come along an' see you when they get time.'

'That'll be bully of 'em, Burt,' said Ron, a little sarcasticaily. Then he shot out: 'What's on your mind?'

'The Old Man insisted I delivered this personally.' Burt fumbled in his shirt, brought forth a bulky brown envelope. 'He's sending you your time, Ron. Here's all the money you got coming to you.'

With his good hand Ron took the envelope. 'Thanks,' he said, and smiled. It was not a nice smile.

'This wasn't my idea y'understand, Ron,' said Burt quickly. 'I didn't want to come here under these circumstances. But you know what the Old Man is – I had to obey orders.'

'Oh, sure, Burt. Sure. Have some coffee.' Ron placed the cash envelope on the bed beside him. He poured out the coffee, handed Burt a cup.

Burt mumbled, 'Thanks'. He looked about him as if he wanted to put the cup down again, but he couldn't find a place so he began to sip the hot liquid.

After a moment he balanced the cup in his hand again and said: 'The Old Man told me to tell you to send for your stuff. He doesn't want you near the place again. He even suggests that you might leave town as soon as you're fit enough.'

'Oh, he does, does he!' Ron's cup rattled, spots of coffee fell on the counterpane. 'Now would you mind taking a message back to your boss, Mr Cooley?'

'This ain't my doing. You've got no call . . .'

'Ain't your doing, hell! Tell the Old Man that I'll leave him to crow on his dungheap. I never want to see it again. But I don't intend to leave town until I find out who killed Duke . . .'

'That's our job.'

'Take it on then.' The voice now was full of cold fury. 'But keep out of my way . . . Keep out of my way.'

The foreman put his half-empty cup on the floor and rose. 'That fight you had must've knocked you crazy.'

'Get out of here!'

Burt Cooley went.

Ron felt himself trembling with rage. He held up his right hand, like a misshapen white paw. That shook too. His gun-hand. His gun-hand should never shake.

He wanted to go out and prove that his gun-hand did not shake. He wanted to blast this filthy town wide open.

He plucked at the bandages savagely. Then his common-sense reasserted himself. The doc had told him that he must not on any account remove the bandages: if he wanted the use of his right hand again he must be patient.

His shoulder began to throb now and, with a whispered curse, he lowered the injured member. The knife-thrust in the fleshy part of the shoulder was already mending and only plagued him when he lifted his arm. But it was his hand that worried him – his right hand. . . .

He got out of bed and made a few tentative steps

across the room. It was the first time he had walked since they tucked him in. He was a mite wobbly at first, but pretty soon was pacing up and down, thinking furiously. If it could be called thinking! – his mind was going round like a crazy mill-wheel. He suddenly realized that inside the thick white glove of bandages he was attempting to clench and unclench his mutilated fingers. In that moment he relived the night, the way he had grabbed the naked blade, the agony. . . .

Something occurred to him suddenly; he was surprised that it had not occurred to him before.

His opponent, Dobbs, had been stripped to the waist, his trousers tightly-belted. He hadn't had a weapon. Surely he could not have kept a knife hidden in his trousers anywhere: it would have been a greater danger to himself than his opponent.

Somebody must have handed him the knife. Duke had slugged him. Duke had been keeping his eye on the two other members of the trio, Messrs. Spingle and Crane. One of these must have slipped the knife to Dobbs during the melee, when Dobbs had been precipitated into the crowd. Duke would maybe have been able to confirm this – but suddenly Ron realized that Duke would not be able to contirm anything anymore. A lump rose to his throat: it was hard to realize that the dapper, volatile little cowhand was dead.

Somebody would pay for it, though. Spingle and Crane came into the running – yeh, and so did Dobbs. Those three were partly to blame for what had happened, even if neither of them had pulled the trigger of the gun that killed Duke – though maybe one of them had!

He hopped back into bed when he heard footsteps on the stairs. Presently Tombstone Mike's cheery voice called, 'Lady to see yuh, suh! May she come in?'

'Sure!'

The door opened and Maria entered.

The sight of her gave him new heart. She asked him how he was, told him her dad had gone out to the Loop V for a final dicker with the Old Man.

'He says your boss asks a mighty high price for his beef, even though it is the best. He says if the old goat doesn't drop his price today he isn't going to do business with him.'

'Good for Jeff. But you'll go back home empty-handed, then, won't you?'

'I guess so.'

'I hope you don't go before you and I have a chance to go riding together.'

'So do I,' she said frankly. 'Still, even if the deal does fall through I think I can persuade Dad to stay a while. He'll be wanting to know how you're going on, too.'

'How are things back home?'

'Fine. Just fine. We've grown a lot since you left us, you know.'

'That seems a long, long time ago.' He glanced at her admiringly and she dropped her head, rummaging in the shopping basket she had laid beside her chair.

Finally she came up with a bag of fruit, smiling impishly. 'We must feed the donkey.'

He raised his wounded hand, threateningly, but had to drop it again. It pleased him to note the look of concern that clouded her face.

'Don't try to overdo things,' she said. 'Don't try too hard.'

'I'll be chasing you down main street in a coupla days,' he threatened as she rose.

'I'll have to go,' she said. 'I've some more shopping to do before dad gets back.' And, with that, she left him.

Mike came up to collect the tray, a pensive look on his face. 'Y'know,' he said. 'Ever since I first saw that Dobbs character I've been trying to figure where I've seen him before. Now I've suddenly remembered. . . .'

'Wal – go on!'

'It ain't that I've seen him before – but that I used to know somebody who he looks very much like. Only this character was older. D'you remember my mentioning a cowhand named Straker – a fast one with a gun – who rode with the Old Man when he first came to town.'

'Yeh, sure. You described him as the fastest thing with a gun you had ever seen. He got bushwhacked or somep'n didn't he?'

'Yeh, him an' his two pards. Nobody was ever pulled in for it. An' young Dobbs is a dead ringer for Straker. A lot younger than Straker was, of course, but big, too, and with the same look to his jib.'

'D'yuh think mebbe they were related?'

'Could be. Though Dobbs would only be a kid when Straker died.'

'If his real name is Dobbs.'

'Yeh.' Now Mike had awakened the younger man's interest, his own interest in the subject seemed to wane. 'Maybe it's just a coincidence,' he said. 'Or maybe I was mistaken. Old age creepin' up, y'know.'

'Hell!' burst out Ron Purcell. 'You keep talkin' about being old. You ain't old. You ain't gettin' enough exercise that's what's the matter with you. Though you won't admit it, you're still hankering for the trail. When I'm feeling less like a spavined mule, you an' me will go an' do a little fiddle-footing.'

'Wa-al,' said Mike doubtfully.

Then he smacked his thigh. 'Yeh. Sure. I'll hold you to that, young fellah.'

'You won't have to remind me.' Ron promised, as the older man left the room.

The man in the bed began to think about Dobbs. He got out of bed, managed to get into his pants, sat in the chair beside the bed.

He felt stronger now, and his thoughts were correspondingly stronger, more disciplined than they had been a short time before. He had another go at pacing the room. Things were beginning to fit in, to make a pattern, a whole.

There was another knock on the door. Ron combed back his hair with his hand and called 'Come in'. It was Jeff Laing.

'Wal, the fightin' man's on his feet again,' crowed the old-timer.

'Sit down, boss,' said Ron sardonically.

Jeff took the chair. Ron sat on the edge of the bed.

Jeff said: 'I heard a rumour you didn't have a boss any more.'

'You heard right. How did you make out with the Old Man – did yuh buy up his spread?'

'Nope. He wouldn't lower his prices. He seemed to think I'd pay anything because I'd come such a long way for the critturs. But I can go elsewhere. I don't aim to be gypped.' Jeff took out a packet of store-cigarettes, handed them across. Ron took one. They lit up.

They didn't talk much after that. Even when Ron had been only a boy, almost a son of Jeff's, they had never needed to say much to each other. Now it was as if the years had been washed away: they still understood each other.

It was not until Jeff had risen to take his leave that he said casually, 'Oh, I almost forgot to tell you – there was a bit of a shindig at the Loop V last night.'

'What kind of a shindig?'

'Somebody set a barn an' a couple of hayricks on fire. A boy was burned pretty badly.'

'A boy. Not Happy, the Indian boy?'

'Yes. The doc says he'll live, but he'll never be the same again. His pardner, Pinto Charlie, is going half-crazy with rage.'

'Charlie's mighty fond of Happy,' said Ron slowly. 'We all are if it comes to that.'

'His face was badly burned,' said Jeff, not realizing what an effect this sentence would have on his listener.

Ron thought of Happy's grinning, good-natured

face as he had known it and shuddered. Then he became filled with a cold rage at the people who had been responsible for the outrage.

'They didn't catch anybody,' said Jeff, thus confirming the younger man's suspicions. And, with that, he left him to his thoughts.

The following day Ron was practising a cross-arm draw with his left hand when Mike yelled that Doc Logan was on his way up.

Ron whipped off his gun-belt, tucked it under the eiderdown, perched himself on the edge of the bed.

The first thing Ron asked was how Happy was faring. The Doc was in a hurry: all he could say was that the Indian lad was doing as well as could be expected. He inspected Ron's shoulder and replaced the bandages with a plaster. 'That'll be all right when the stiffness wears off,' he said.

Ron poked his hand forward impatiently and the Doc took the wrappings from that, too.

'Hm, yes. Clean. Quite clean. I'll put a plaster on that, too. But don't try to pick things up or anything like that or you'll bust it up again.'

'Is it gonna be all right?'

'I think so. A good job you're made of seasoned leather.'

And the young man had to be content with that.

As soon as the doc had left, he dressed himself completely, except for his gun-belt, and went downstairs. But, for a while, he kept pretty much out of sight.

And so the days passed.

One morning he went downstairs and learned from Mike that the little drummer, Septimus B. Jones, had been in the saloon.

'Heck! Why didn't you tell me. I'd kind of like to have a talk with that little gink.'

'You'll have your chance. He usually stops in town coupla three days.' Mike went on to his next item of news. 'The Old Man had some more beef rustled last night.'

'Anybody hurt?'

'Nope.'

'Good. I don't care whether the Old Man's left without a single dogie as long as none of my old saddle-mates don't get hurt.'

But things were certainly coming to a head, Ron reflected silently. He flexed his fingers in their tapes. Another couple of days and he figured the hand would be as good as new.

CHAPTER XII

Jacko Chubbs, the town fool, was grooming a horse in the livery-stables. He was handling the job while the hostler laid up with a bad case of rheumatism in his back. He was alone in the half-dusk, except for the horse, and he liked horses. He liked to be alone, too. When he was alone he could talk to himself (in this case he talked to the horse), could build around himself that little world of makebelieve that the others (the sly ones!) could not penetrate.

He wore his new hat, his black, beautiful sombrero, pushed to the back of his head. It was at strange variance with his rags.

A shadow fell across the open doorway of the stable, blocking out the late afternoon sunlight. Half-apprehensively, Jacko slowly turned his head.

The other man came further into the stables and finally Jacko recognized him and was relieved.

'Howdy, Mistuh Purcell.'

'Howdy, Jacko. How are things with you?'

'Fine. Sure. Fine.' Jacko liked Mr Purcell: he wasn't one of the sly ones.

Jacko wrinkled his brow in an effort of memory and finally he asked, 'Is your arm better, Mistuh Purcell?'

'Yes, it's fine, thanks, Jacko.'

'I seed your fight, Mistuh Purcell. It wuz a corker. You had that big fellah beat, he wuz a skunk to pull a knife the way he did.'

Now, Ron figured, was his chance. But easily – easily. 'Say, Jacko,' he said casually. 'I've bin admiring your sombrero. What made you pick a hat like that?'

Jacko stroked, lovingly, the wide brim of the black sombrero. The association of ideas which was already implanted in his mind made it easy for him to answer the question. 'That man you fought, Mistuh Purcell, I seed him wearin' one jus' like this.'

'The big young man I fought? Are you sure it was him? Are you sure it wasn't one of his two pardners who was wearing the hat?'

Jacko scowled as if Ron was arguing with him. 'It wuz the young one all right. I remember well.'

'Sure yuh do, Jacko,' said Ron soothingly. 'When was this you saw him wearing the hat? I ain't seen him wearing one like that.'

'Mebbe he lost it.'

Maybe he did, reflected Ron, savagely sardonic. And Jacko went on:

'I went to meet the stage to carry bags for the people. The big one got off the stage first. I carried his bag an' he gave me two bits. I didn't like him then – two bits ain't much an' them was mighty heavy bags. Mr Sep was on the stage an' I could've got more money off him if I'd've known. But he wuz last – that bozo an' his two pardners got off before Mr Sep an' Mr Sep carried his own bags an' I didn't see him till he got in the hotel an' then the clerk got his bags – ever'body knows Mr Sep pays well . . .'

Jacko dried up, stopped for breath. Although Ron's next question was almost choking him as he let it come out slowly. 'You mean Mr Sep Jones the salesman who comes to town from time to time, don't you, Jacko?'

'Sure. He comes from the city. He ain't like the folks out here. You know him, Mistuh Purcell?'

'I guess so.'

'He came into town again the other day. I carried his bags this time. He gave me a silver dollar.'

'Is he still at the hotel?'

'Ye-es.' Jacko began to scowl a bit more.

But he brightened remarkably when the young man gave him another silver dollar, before striding out into the dying glow of the late afternoon.

Jacko bit the silver dollar before placing it carefully into a pocket of his tattered vest. He continued grooming the horse. It was dark in the stable now, but Jacko did not need light. He talked to himself as he worked.

Meanwhile Ron Purcell entered the commercial hotel and asked if Septimus B. Jones was available. The rat-faced clerk said he was, then asked Ron if his wounds were better. Ron said, 'Yes, thanks,' reflecting sardonically as he climbed the stairs that people were very concerned about his health all of a sudden.

He found Sep Jones in the process of shaving, one half of his round, pink face plastered with lather. He was in his shirt sleeves and his suspenders were of a violent purple. He wore natty pin-stripe trousers and red leather slippers. He wiped his face with a beautifully-clean multi-coloured towel and twinkled at his visitor as he looked him up and down.

'You're Mr Ron Purcell I guess.'

'How did you know?'

'A mutual friend of ours described you to me. Also you still have sticking-plaster on one of your fingers.' He twinkled some more. 'What can I do for you, Mr Purcell. I don't expect you want to buy any ladies' undergarments do you?'

'Not just now, thank you. To tell you the truth, I'm more interested in hats.'

Septimus spread his hands. 'I haven't got a single hat with me at the moment.'

'Didn't you deliver a few more lush black Mexican-like sombreros to the man at the emporium?'

'Oh, I see. No, there's been such a rush on that particular line that I couldn't get any this time. Why, did the man promise you one?'

'Kinda. Tell me, Mr Jones. Do you remember the last time you came to Rampage – you travelled in the stage with three gentleman who called themselves cattle-buyers.'

'Yes, sure, they're still staying here in the hotel.'

'And you sold one of them a hat?'

'Yes. I had a spare sample with me and Mr Dobbs admired it so I sold it him at cost-price. A real bargain. I'm afraid, however, I haven't one I could let you have cost price, Mr Purcell.'

Ron eyed him speculatively, wondering if the little cuss was trying to be funny. But Septimus still twinkled guilelessly.

'Thank you for the information, Mr Jones.'

Mr Jones twinkled a little less. 'Might I ask why you wanted the information, Mr Purcell?'

'You might,' said Mr Purcell. 'But I cain't give you an answer right now. Maybe in two or three days, huh?'

Mr Jones held up his hand, palm outwards Indian fashion. 'Huh,' he said humorously. But he still was not twinkling at full power again.

Mr Purcell left him, went downstairs, out into the street. It was dusk now. Mr Purcell flexed his right hand meditatively. Then he went back to Tombstone Mike's place to fetch his gun-belt.

Mr Dobbs was feeling quite fit again. This particular evening he was alone, his two pardners having business elsewhere. He had heard that Ron Purcell was up and about again, probably thirsting for Mr Dobbs's blood. What could a man with a gammy hand do? Mr Dobbs, however, had heard a rumour that Purcell's hand – and his shoulder, too – were all right again. Mr Dobbs wasn't scared of Purcell – no, sir – still, he was wise enough to take precautions against being taken unawares: even if Purcell's gammy right hand was *not* all right again, maybe he could shoot just as straight with his left one.

So Mr Dobbs took precautions. For instance, he didn't enter Lemmy's Place by the batwings anymore. That way a man was silhouetted against the light for longer than was absolutely comfortable, particularly if the man expected to have hot lead spewed at him at any moment. So Mr Dobbs glanced through the window of the saloon and, although he saw no danger, to be on the safe side he turned about and around the corner and approached the side door in the alley.

But he never reached it.

What had at first been an immovable shadow became suddenly an animated black figure and, before Dobbs could turn, a gun-barrel was rammed into his side and a husky voice said, 'Take it easy, pardner.'

Dobbs's belly turned to ice; the ice spread, freezing his limbs. He felt suddenly naked as his forty-five was neatly lifted from its holster.

'March, pardner,' said the voice, and, like an automaton, Dobbs marched.

Around the dark backs of Rampage a silent party of horsemen awaited Dobbs and his captor. The latter turned out to be Tombstone Mike. There was a horse waiting for each of them, and Dobbs was forced to mount. Nobody said a word. The cavalcade moved off.

Now Dobbs began to recognize others of the party. Ron Purcell, Jeff Laing; a few more of Tombstone

Mike's friends and other townsfolk; and, perhaps strangest of all under the circumstances, Sheriff Sam Brighouse.

'What's this?' said Dobbs. 'What's the idea?'

Nobody answered him. They did not even look at him, but they hemmed him in like a ring of steel.

As they moved into the open the wind made itself felt, blustering and grumbling from out on the range. The sky was overcast. There was no moon and what few stars appeared were so infinitesimal that they gave no light at all. There was threat of a storm. . . . Suddenly even the elements seemed to range themselves against Dobbs, their atmosphere matching that of the riders.

'What's the game?' Dobbs said. 'By God, I'll yell, if . . .'

Something hard and cold was jabbed into his side but still nobody spoke. All that could be heard was the clop-clop of the horses' hooves, and even this was drowned from time to time by the blustering of the wind.

Slowly from in the distance thunder rolled.

Dobbs shivered.

The horsemen went over a rise and began to descend into a little hollow. Then, before them, Dobbs saw the bare group of trees like waiting executioners. That numb, icy feeling came into his stomach again, but he could not even shiver any more.

The horsemen made a circle around the largest tree with its convenient outthrust bough. One of them produced a lariat, shook part of it out.

The circle widened a little then and the man with the lariat moved up to Dobbs, then stopped before he was within arms reach. Dobbs gave a startled exclamation as his arms were suddenly grabbed from behind and forced behind his back. Cold, rough rawhide closed over his wrists, tightened until it cut into the flesh.

The man with the lariat moved forward again, the hangnoose ready. Dobbs jerked forward in the saddle but was again held from behind. The blow of a fist knocked his hat off. The loop was dropped over his head. He yelled then:

'What have I done? Why are you doing this, fellahs? What's the matter with you all?'

Nobody answered him. His head jerked around, his starting eyes sought out the sheriff. 'Sam! Why . . .' He choked as the noose tightened, as the other end of the lariat was slung over the bough.

Sam Brighouse had not spoken either, but now he kneed his horse a little nearer to Dobbs. The latter's eyes implored him, his name escaped again and again from the constricted throat. The sheriff watched dispationately, as if he was court and judge; and executioner, too: he had a new dignity that was almost awe-inspiring. Dobbs knew that a man stood at his side, a quirt raised above the horse's head. He wagged his head, trying desperately to free the noose. And, finally, Sam Brighouse spoke.

'You've got one chance, Dobbs.'

Dobbs nodded his head frantically.

'Loosen the rope,' said the sheriff, and this was done.

The sheriff went on: 'We want to know the truth of everything you and your two pards have cooked up against the Loop V and against the town and we want the names of all your accomplices. We also want to know who killed Walt Crisp, Hank Butler and Duke Linstone.'

'I don't know nothing about all that. I . . .' Dobbs gagged as the rope tightened again.

'All right. String him up,' said the sheriff unemotionally.

A scream burst from the open mouth of the doomed man. Even as they loosened the rope again he was babbling so fast his words did not make sense.

'I knew he was a yellow skunk all along,' said Ron Purcell. 'I figured he was bound to crack eventually.'

Dobbs was gasping for breath now. One of the men pushed a flask to his mouth. Then Sam Brighouse said 'Take it slow. Make sure you tell it all – and right, too, or we're liable to change our minds.'

Trying to keep the quaver out of his voice, Dobbs told his story.

He was the son of Straker, the gunfighter who had ridden with the Old Man in his early days. The Old Man, before he settled in Rampage and became respectable had been a leader of a band of owl-hooters. His name had been Lafe Garnett.

After a running fight with Mexican federals Garnett and his three pards had been the only ones to escape. The three men, of which Straker was by far the most dangerous, were the only ones who knew what the Old Man had been. They had to be killed so Lafe Garnett could be safe forever. Dobbs had only been a kid at the time, waiting, with his mother, for his father to return. The three men, with 'pay-off' money in their pockets, were on their way home when they were bushwhacked. It didn't need a detective to figure out who had instigated this, and why.

Young Dobbs had discovered all this as he came to manhood, fighting around the mining-camps. He could scrap, yes, but he had never been very handy with a gun. So he had to hire men to help him to do what he wanted to do: ruin the Old Man.

He had known Lemmy Macklein as a mining-camp gambler before the snake-like crook hit Rampage. He'd met up with Spingle and Crane in the same way: they were game for any kind of skullduggery. When they figured the time was ripe – the Old Man's empire had swollen until it was ripe for bursting – the three of them got in touch with Lemmy and his boys.

It was Lemmy's idea to bring in Kid Stone, the West's most notorious hired gunfighter. This had been expensive and, right now, Dobbs thought maybe it hadn't been such a good idea after all. The Kid didn't like taking orders and he had some very queer rules of his own making.

Still, things had gone on pretty well, with or without the sick-faced gunman. Two herds of the Old Man's prime cattle had been rustled, taken to the buyer on the other side of the badlands; four of the Old Man's hands had been killed and two of them incapacitated.

But Dobbs had to correct himself there, glancing at Ron Purcell, who looked as right as rain again.

He babbled on, trying to cover himself. Spingle had killed Walt Crisp, or maybe it had been Crane; the old man had put up a fight there on the edge of Mud Hollow. He had had to be silenced anyway because he had spotted the three so-called cattle-buyers reconnoitring the day before and might have put two and two together and talked. Walt Crisp had had to be killed, too, in case Hank Butler had passed on information to his old pard when he visited him in Doc Logan's sick bay.

Lemmy's boy, Mose, had done that job. He was a born killer. He had shot Duke Linstone in the back, too, in revenge for the way the little cowhand had made Lemmy and him look foolish in the saloon brawl. He had also stripped Duke of valuable evidence that the little cowhand had just filched from Lemmy's office.

Dobbs, it seemed, had finished his tale. He had been a man with a mission. A mission that was understandable and natural beneath the code of the West: an eye for an eye, a tooth for a tooth. But he hadn't been a big enough man to carry that mission and it had got tangled in with greed.

'We'll go back to town an' pick up the rest of 'em,' said Sheriff Brighouse.

But Dobbs, after all, had not completely finished. 'You're too late,' he shrilled. 'The boys left for the Loop V before you picked me up. Spingle, Crane, Lemmy, the Kid, Mose, and a big force to back 'em up: they're gonna wipe out the Loop V tonight and run all the cattle off. They wouldn't let me go – they said I ain't fit to ride again yet.' His voice rose to a scream, his eyes glared. 'But I don't care as long as they wipe 'em out, as long . . .'

Sam Brighouse slapped him across the face with a gloved palm, rocking him in the saddle. 'Let's go,' said the sheriff.

Another horseman appeared suddenly over the rise, erect in the saddle, his two guns covering the group.

'Stay put a mite longer, if you please, gentlemen,' said Kid Stone.

One of the men went for his gun. The Kid fired. The man clutched at his shoulder, pitched from the saddle.

'Kid,' babbled Dobbs. 'I thought you . . .'

'You thought wrong, my friend. When the boys were ready to ride I could not be found. So, calling me a yellow dog, they rode without me.'

'Les!' burst out Sheriff Brighouse. 'Why didn't you tell me?'

'Why should I? I don't care if they burn the Loop V to the ground and Garnett with it. I never did like hogs, that's why I took this job. But pretty soon I began to dislike my colleagues and the way they did things. I don't like people who shoot old men, who shoot a man in the back from the darkness. When I kill people I like to do it in my own way.' He chuckled sardonically. 'After all, I have my reputation to consider.'

'How did you find us here, Les?'

'I tailed you. But we mustn't waste time in chatting, must we? Will one of you take the rope from around Dobbs' neck an' untie his hands. Easy! Spread out! Don't crowd!'

The man who had been creased in the shoulder was on his feet again, murmuring that he was all right.

'All right,' echoed Kid Stone. 'Let's give Dobbs a space all to himself.'

'What are yuh gonna do, Kid?' babbled Dobbs. 'What're yuh gonna do.'

'You yeller-livered skunk,' said the Kid. 'I ought to plug you in the guts an' watch you squirm. But I ain't gonna lower myself. Next time you want to play badman pick a punch o' schoolgirls to help you. Get going now. Keep riding. If you cross my patch again I'll surely kill you.'

Dobbs clutched the horse's reins and stared at the Kid as if he could hardly believe his ears. Then he turned the horse, kicked it with his heels. A few seconds later horse and rider disappeared into the night.

'You shouldn't've done that, Les,' said the sheriff. 'You've put yourself in bad again.'

'Ain't I always in bad,' said Kid sardonically. He half-turned his horse, but still his two guns covered the group.

'I'll be in town if anybody wants me,' he said. And with that parting remark he disappeared back over the rise.

Men kneed their horses forward. Sheriff Brighouse seemed bemused. Ron Purcell took over, yelled, 'Let him go! Right now there are more important things. Let's get to the Loop V before it's too late.'

As they rode, the storm broke.

CHAPTER XIII

The Old Man was alone in the ranch-house when the raiders struck. His men, penned in the bunk-house, didn't have a chance to get to him. Spingle and Crane dismounted and went in after him. Spingle got a bullet in the head; Crane retreated in haste.

Meanwhile Lemmy Macklein and his trusty back-shooting pard, Mose, had gotten in the back way. Lemmy had always hated the Old Man. Lemmy wanted to be the only power in the territory and the Old Man stood in the way of that ambition. Lemmy had always coveted the Old Man's land and stock, too; when the gullible Dobbs approached with his plan Lemmy saw in it the chance he had been waiting for.

He was a mite too hasty now, though: he should have left the back-shooting caper to Mose, who had had more experience. The Old Man whirled, beat Lemmy to the shot and blasted him down to die horribly with two bullets in his stomach . . .

But Mose was already fanning the hammer of his

gun; and the Old Man died before he could fire another shot.

Mose picked up a heavy brass candlestick and threw it at the lamp, smashing it, spraying burning oil over the room. Then he ran.

The place was soon ablaze, a fitting funeral-pyre for the two arch-princes of greed.

The raiders concentrated on the bunk-house. The storm which had been threatening so long suddenly broke. It was too late to put out the fire at the ranch-house – now crumbling to black ruins – but it prevented the fire from spreading to the bunk-house and the besieged cowhands there had a brief respite.

Lightning flashes fitfully illumined the raiders as they rode Indian-fashion round and round the bunk-house. Curtained by the driving rain they were like demons, and very hard to hit. They were able to get close to the windows before they could be seen. They poured withering fire through the windows.

The first victim inside was the cook. He fell dead with blood gushing from a wound in his throat. Charlie Pinto evened the score by picking off the man who had done the job. The raiders moved out a little, once more. No doubt they figured they would eventually wear resistance down. They would have been jubilant had they known that the besieged garrison was getting short of ammunition. All the spare stuff was kept in the lean-to by the ranch-house. The flames had not managed to blow this up but it was too far away to be reached. Anybody who tried to reach it through that cordon of riding demons would be simply committing suicide.

The men held their shots, trying to make each one tell. But the rain, which maybe had saved them from the fire, was against them now in disguising the movements of their opponents.

Out there Mose was ramrodding things now. This was the kind of chance he had waited for all his life and he was making the most of it. When this was finished *he* would be the boss of Rampage territory!

He howled with rage when Ron Purcell and his band suddenly descended on them from out of the storm.

That night, Rampage territory really lived up to its name. The battle at the Loop V – and what followed it – was something that was talked about for countless years afterwards, a tale that old-timers mumbled in their baccy-stained beards as the lawless West was dying. It continues to be told now, though most of those who participated in it are long since dead and Rampage is a ghost-town in which coyotes prowl and the winds – the same tearing winds that blew that night – play merry with the sagebrush and the sand and the stunted prairie grass.

As the Ron Purcell faction swept down like avenging angels in the lightning and the rain, Mr Crane was the first to fall, a bullet in his heart. The three 'cattle-buyers' hadn't done so very well out of the Rampage caper after all. Two of them dead – and one body already burnt to a crisp – the third fleeing with his tail between his legs, branded a coward, fearful of showing his face in good company again. Nobody ever found out what actually happened to

Dobbs, although it was surmised that he went East and changed his name, the way his father, Straker, had changed his before him. He probably finished up as a drink-sodden bouncer in some filthy dive or flophouse in 'Frisco or Chicago.

Mose, however, the late Lemmy's successor, was made of sterner stuff. He rallied his men and they made a run for it. Some of them, Mose among them, managed, in the confusion and the storm, to get past the Ron Purcell faction.

But the latter were soon on their heels and a running fight developed. The demoralized Rampage toughs split up in all directions, seeking to escape in the storm. All they wanted to do was get away from the territory with a whole skin and never be seen there any more. A few of them succeeded. Others were picked off as they tried to escape. The Rampage 'vigilantes' were utterly merciless. This was the stuff of legend to go down in history, plenty of blood and horror and merciless carnage.

A bunch of five hard cases kept on for town. Maybe they had treasures there.

One of them, indeed, thought he might at least *find* treasures there: he was staking his life and liberty on one last desperate bid. This was Mose. He had a good horse and he streaked ahead of the others. He knew where Lemmy kept the cash and, if he possibly could, he meant to escape from town with as much of it as he could carry.

He thundered into town with the other four at his heels. One of them, badly wounded, suddenly fell in the dust. There were more people on the sidewalks than might have been expected. They looked scared, too, as well they might be.

As the four riders moved towards the saloon a man shouted, 'Kid Stone's in there. He's taken it over – he turned us all out.'

Mose reined in. 'Go get him,' he said, and the three men, accustomed to taking orders, dismounted and moved on.

One of them took the batwings, the other two took a window apiece. One of them died almost immediately. He was bold: he got too close to the window and a slug came through it and almost took the top of his head off.

The other two rushed the batwings and managed to get inside: they wanted to be heroes; maybe they knew what Mose had in mind and wanted to cut themselves into the dinero.

Mose followed them. The shooting became fast and furious.

Blue gunsmoke drifted through the gently-swinging batwings. The shooting died and there was a hush. Then the batwings swung a little faster and a man staggered out. He did a little buck and wing on the edge of the boardwalk before falling flat on his face in the dust.

The batwings swung more slowly again – slowly – until they weren't swinging at all and Lemmy's Place was as silent as the grave.

It was still that way when Ron Purcell and his boys rode in and had the exciting news thrown at them by the dogs – lame or yellow – who had stayed at home to bury the dead.

Maria Laing ran out to her father, who was bleeding from the arm.

'Oh, Dad, you shouldn't've gone with them. It wasn't your affair.'

'You don't mean that, honey,' said old Jeff.

The girl lowered her head. 'No, I guess I don't.' And when she raised it again she was not looking at her father any more but at Ron Purcell, who rode beside him.

'You better get off the street, Maria,' said the young man gravely. 'There's liable to be some more shooting.'

'Do as he says, honey,' said the father.

The girl looked at them, one after the other. 'Look after yourselves, both of you,' she said. Then she left them.

The men began to dismount, range themselves opposite Lemmy's Place, getting near cover in case they needed it. Then, from inside the saloon, a voice rang out.

'Ron Purcell! Is Ron Purcell there?'

'I'm here, Kid. What do you want?'

'There's one other living man in here besides myself. He ain't got a mark on him. His name's Mose an' he's the man who shot your pard, Duke, in the back. I'm giving him his gun back and sending him out to yuh. He's all yours. Take him.'

'I'll take him,' said Ron Purcell, but only those near to him heard the words.

Mose came out running, his gun leaping to his hand. He found himself covered by a battery of weapons.

'Gimme a chance,' he shouted hoarsely. 'Don't shoot me down like a dog.'

'You're getting a chance,' said Ron Purcell. 'A better one than you deserve. Put your gun back. I'll come out to meet you. If you get me you'll be given a chance to get away.'

Mose holstered his gun, stepped slowly from the boardwalk. The lean man with the scarred face came from the other side of the street to meet him.

It was all over in a split second. Mose went for his gun first, but was a fraction too slow. Ron Purcell fired only one shot. The heavy slug slammed Mose in the chest, knocking him backwards, his toes upturned.

The echoes died. 'So now there's only Kid Stone left,' said Jeff Laing softly.

'I never figured he'd come back here an' wait like he said,' breathed Sam Brighouse.

'I figured he would,' said Ron Purcell. 'The Kid has a strange code – part of it is that he always keeps his word.'

'Wal, I guess I better go get him out,' said Sam Brighouse, and began to walk.

'Wait, Sam.' Ron Purcell started after him.

An old townsman, one of Sam's contemporaries, grabbed Ron's arm. 'You'll have to let him go, son. He's been shamed enough. After all, he's still sheriff, you know.'

'You're right,' said Ron Purcell. He stood back with the others, watched Sheriff Brighouse pass through the batwings. They were still swinging when the single shot rang out.

Sam came back slowly, step by step. He turned and they saw that he was unarmed now. He clutched his right wrist, from which blood dripped sluggishly.

There was shame and pain in his eyes and the lines in his face were grey and old as he retraced his steps. 'I never figured Les would do that to me,' he said.

Ron Purcell's voice rang out. 'I guess it's you and me now, Kid.'

'I'm waiting for you, Ron,' shouted Kid Stone. 'Both my irons are cased.'

When he entered the bar-room he could not at first see his man because all the lights had been put out except a single one over the bar. Then he realized that the Kid had placed himself directly beneath the light so that he could not, in fact, be missed at all.

He was standing negligently with his elbows on the bar, a half-empty glass of liquor by one of them.

'I'm sorry it had to be this way, Ron,' he said.

'So am I. It had to happen sooner or later though, I guess.'

'I'm proud to have known you, Ron.'

'Likewise, Kid.'

The Kid straightened up, moved a little way away from the bar.

'Let's go, pardner,' he said.

Ron Purcell walked slowly nearer, so that he too was in the light, so that he could not gain any advantage from the shadows. They faced each other, these two men, so dissimilar, yet so strangely alike.

They watched each other's eyes, as all good gunfighters do, and which one made the first movement could never have been determined, for it was as if some silent signal passed between them and they went for their guns.

The Kid was spun half-around by the slug that smashed his shoulder in the blast and the flame. He straightened around and tried to lift his other gun but it was suddenly too heavy for him. He let it fall beside its twin. He clutched at his shoulder, the broken bone, the thick blood oozing sluggishly through his fingers.

He had to lean against the bar to prevent himself from falling. He had not fired a shot.

His sick fading eyes mirrored disbelief, but no fear. He gathered his strength to scream:

'Kill me! Goddam you – kill me!'

'I'll send the Doc in to fix you up,' said Ron Purcell. 'After that, get out of town. Good luck, Kid.'

He turned on his heels. Kid Stone did not answer him.

Half-an-hour later he did as he was told and left town. His proud soul was humbled, his legend laid forever. The West saw him no more. There was a rumour that he got killed a couple of years later fighting a civil war in Cuba, a soldier of fortune to the last.

Maria Laing met Ron Purcell as he walked out into the street. And it was she who, an hour later, led her young man to the hotel room where her father awaited them.

'Sit down, son,' grinned old Jeff. 'I hope you don't mind me calling you son.'

'No, suh.'

'I allus hoped I might do some day,' said the old man softly. He looked enquiringly at his daughter. She said:

'No, I haven't said anything to him about it, I figured I'd leave that for you. But, don't worry, it's all right.' She reached out and took Ron's hand. He said:

'What's all the mystery?' But he had probably already guessed what it was all about.

'I need a new foreman, son,' said Jeff. 'How about coming back with us and filling the post?'

'What about the foreman you've already got?'

'He's getting kinda old. I promised I'd pension him off as soon as I got a younger man good enough to take his place. He won't mind being let out to grass. What do you say, Ron?'

'I say all right, boss.' The young man grinned. 'But what's the pay?'

'Good enough.'

'How about bonus?'

'Seems to me you've already got your bonus,' said Jeff with a chuckle.

Ron looked enquiringly at Maria and she winked, cheekily.

They both looked at old Jeff and the next moment all three of them were laughing fit to raise the roof.